DEAD FOR LIFE

DEAD FOR LIFE

Dead For Good Book Five

STACY CLAFLIN

NOLON KING

STERLING & STONE

Chapter One

Knock, knock!

Brad Morris quickly slammed the drawer and stood up straight. He couldn't help feeling like he was doing something wrong every time he went through Kurt's desk.

Except that desk now belonged to Brad.

He squared his shoulders and answered the door.

Scott stood on the other side. His eyes widened. "Brad? What are you doing in here?"

"Someone has to run this place now that Kurt's locked away." And Bancroft had managed to make it look like Brad had attempted to interfere with Kurt's arrest, so that Ralf would have more reason to trust him. He stepped back, giving the older assassin room to come inside, then he closed the door behind them. "It's great to see you. Have you healed enough to come back to work?"

"I'm up for researching targets or training new assassins. We can talk later about me possibly returning to the field." Scott took the seat Brad usually did when coming in to talk with Kurt. "You're really running the show now?"

It had been over a month now, but he still felt like an imposter taking over the boss's office.

Brad sat across from the man who'd been somewhat of a mentor when Brad first joined the business. "Ralf always runs things, whether he's here or not."

"He probably checks in on you daily, I'd imagine."

"Not as much as I'd expect, but then again, he's busy trying to free Kurt."

Scott's expression turned serious. "Do you think this is a good time to get out of the business? A lot of people have been going down this year."

"Rose and Kurt both had it coming," Brad said quickly.

They'd both tried to take him down, both had tried to kill him. Should've known better than to go after one of the top assassins in the business.

Scott leaned forward. "I have to say, I'm surprised that Ralf gave you the position."

It felt surreal to Brad, too.

But it was precisely the position he needed. Now that Kurt had revealed that Ralf was the one to put the hit on his dad's life, Brad would have the opportunity to get close enough to kill him. He'd gotten into the assassin business to eventually find and take down the man who murdered his father.

The last thing he ever imagined was that he'd end up working for them.

Yet here he was. Now it was only a matter of patience. Waiting for the right opportunity.

Then he could finally avenge his father's death.

He turned his attention back to Scott. "If you hadn't gotten injured, it might've been you. You're not going to try to take my job, are you?"

They both laughed.

Scott had never had any interest in running the business. He loved the thrill of pursuit. How long he'd keep it up was up in the air. He was already in his sixties and had gotten injured on his last job.

If Brad were in his shoes, he'd be thinking about slowing down. Focusing more on other aspects of their line of work.

Probably why he wanted to do research and training. Aside from retirement, there weren't other options — unless he ended up in jail or dead. That was where so many others found themselves before fifty. Sometimes much sooner.

Brad shuffled some papers. "Are you ready to start today? Or just dropping in?"

"I'm eager to get back to it. What do you have for me?"

"You up for putting away stock? I haven't had time myself, and there aren't many I can trust with it. If you know what I mean."

Scott nodded. "Sensitive material."

"Precisely."

"Glad to help. I used to do some of the inventory way back before you took it over."

"You mean around the time dinosaurs went extinct?"

They laughed again.

It was good to have Scott back. Felt like a lifetime since he'd worked with someone at his level.

"Any boxes you want me to start with?" Scott headed for the door.

"No. If you need help with the lifting, holler. Or let one of the kids out front know."

"I'll be fine."

Brad breathed a sigh of relief as Scott closed the door between them. He was someone Brad could trust with his life. There weren't many left that he could say that about.

He returned to his real job — digging up dirt on the Bergmanns. Ralf had all but disappeared after giving Brad his son's old office and responsibilities. Now the older man's focus was tied between the business and freeing his son.

Kurt would never see the outside of a prison if Agent June Bancroft had her way. She'd already tied Kurt to the deaths of several overseas political leaders that had affected American politics.

His face was all over social media.

It was a PR nightmare. But not something Brad needed to worry about. Ralf had put others on that job.

Brad just needed to keep the knife shop running as a cover and assign targets to the other assassins. For the time being, he didn't have to do any kills himself now that he had Kurt's job.

But working for two bosses — Ralf and the agent — was like walking a tightrope made of human hair over a fiery pit of spikes.

The agent did not want Brad to allow the killings of any political leaders or businessmen. And now Brad knew that was almost every target in the company, despite the lies he'd been fed all these years about killing criminals who'd gotten away from justice in the system.

He returned a few phone calls, and before he knew it, his phone's alarm went off.

It was time to visit his daughter in the mental hospital.

Chapter Two

BRAD'S BREATH hitched as they neared Hadley's room. It was anyone's guess what they would see when the nurse opened the door.

They were allowed to see her today, so that was a good sign. She'd had more good days than bad recently.

Hopefully soon, her doctor would release her to come home to her real room, which she hadn't seen in over a month.

The nurse turned to him and Faye before unlocking the door. "I'm not sure what Dr. Fallow told you, but she's resting. It's been a busy day."

"What do you mean by busy?" Faye demanded.

Brad gave her hand a gentle squeeze.

The nurse hesitated. "She spent a good deal of time in the art center painting."

"Is there a problem with what she made?" Brad asked.

"It was rather bloody. Crimson splashes all over."

His stomach knotted. If Hadley confessed to accidentally killing Nate, even the agent's promise of immunity might not be enough to keep her out of prison. Word would get out, people would demand justice.

Faye's grip tightened on his hand. "She lost her baby in a bloody mess, and her boyfriend was murdered. What do you expect from her? Sunshine and kittens? She isn't here because her life is perfect. Can you imagine going through that kind of grief at such a young age?"

The nurse took a deep breath. "The picture disturbed some of the other patients."

"Maybe you should let Hadley paint in her own room," Faye snapped. "Did you think of that?"

"That isn't a bad idea," Brad agreed. He tried to see around the nurse into the window of his daughter's room.

"Certain items aren't allowed in the patients' rooms." The nurse frowned. "Come inside, and if you have any questions, you should direct them to her doctor."

Faye's brows furrowed. "I want to see her painting, see if it's as bad as you make out."

"Take it up with Dr. Fallow." The nurse opened the door and poked her head in. "Hadley, you have guests."

Brad let Faye go inside first, then he followed her in. The white room had more color than in times past. Hadley had taped several paintings above the bed. None were bloody or morbid.

Faye let go of his hand and threw her arms around Hadley, who sat on the bed with a book.

"I'll make sure Dr. Fallow knows you're here." The nurse left, closing the door.

Brad sat next to Hadley and put his hand on her shoulder. "How are you doing?"

No matter how many times they visited, it was always jolting to see her with dark circles under her eyes and ratty hair. His daughter was a girl who never left the bathroom with a hair out of place or with makeup less than perfect.

She was even thinner than before, and she'd never had much weight to spare.

Hadley sighed dramatically. "They won't let me do anything."

"Like what?" Faye asked.

"Anything. All I ever do is sit in here, go to group therapy, go to counseling with Dr. Fallow, and eat. Class sometimes, but not often enough. The only interesting one is art, and they won't let me draw what I want."

Brad motioned toward the paintings on the walls. "Those are nice."

"They're boring."

Faye put her arm around Hadley. "What did you draw today?"

Hadley wrinkled her nose. "What did Nurse Ratched tell you?"

Brad held back a snicker. "She said some of the other patients weren't thrilled with your artwork."

"What else am I supposed to draw? The instructor said to put the images from our minds onto the page. That's what I did."

Faye whispered, "You haven't told anyone about … you know?"

They all knew.

Hadley had killed her classmate Nate, and he and Faye helped to cover it up. And now the agent had a fall guy already arrested for the crime.

But if Hadley confessed, people would believe her. Everyone had pointed fingers at her because of the argument she'd had with Nate shortly before his death. He'd followed her around town — stalked her — and then confronted her in a dark park, shortly after his dad had threatened her.

She'd felt attacked. How was she supposed to react?

"Well?" Faye asked.

"I'm not telling anyone."

Brad exchanged a look with his wife. Hadley had so much pressing on her psyche — her boyfriend's murder, the loss of the baby that she saw as her only remaining connection to him, and accidentally killing her friend. It was more than most adults would be able to handle. All it would take was a slip of the tongue to the wrong person.

"Have you talked about the other stuff?" Faye held Hadley's hands in her own.

"Over and over. Talking about it doesn't help. Being here doesn't help. Neither do the drugs they make me take."

"How do they make you feel?" Brad asked. "Talkative?"

She shook her head. "The opposite. Tired. And they make me feel less. Not that they could take away all the pain. When do I get to go home?"

Faye wrapped her arms around Hadley. "Dr. Fallow and Dr. Trellis both think you're better off here, getting the help you need in dealing with the grief."

Hadley scowled. "They just want to punish me for attacking the nurses when I first got here."

"They aren't," Brad assured her. "Everyone wants to see you make a full recovery."

"I could do that at home."

"You're getting daily counseling here. Like you said, group and individual. That couldn't happen at home. We only see Dr. Trellis weekly."

"It doesn't help!" Tears shone in her eyes. "I can talk about losing Duke and the baby, and even about Nate's 'disappearance,' but you know what? No amount of talking will bring them back. Nobody's coming back! And to make matters worse, Ellie still hates me."

Faye patted her arm. "I'm sure she's had plenty of time to cool down."

"No. Lucy has visited me three times. Do you think Ellie has? No, because she's mad at me for not telling her that I was seeing Duke. She knows I'm crushed about his death, but she doesn't care. Only that I never told her. And now she has the lead in the school play. She took my role. And not once has my 'best friend' asked how I am."

Brad grimaced. No wonder his daughter was falling apart.

She'd lost everything important to her, except for her family. And she hadn't asked about anyone since she was admitted.

"Luna keeps asking about you." Brad pulled out a paper from his jacket and unfolded it. "She drew this for you."

Hadley's expression softened as she looked at the crayon-drawn picture of rainbow-colored ponies.

Faye rested her head on Hadley's shoulder. "Grandma and Zeke are eager to see you, too."

"How much do they know?"

"Grandma and Luna never knew about the pregnancy, so we haven't told them about the loss. Zeke knew, so we told him."

"He probably thinks I'm a huge loser now."

"No. He's worried about you."

"Everyone wants you to come home soon," Brad added.

Hadley frowned. "Am I ever getting out of here?"

"Do you *want* to?" he asked.

Her eyes narrowed slightly. "Why wouldn't I?"

"You haven't shown any progress — to us or the staff here. You really need to try."

"And then I can go home?"

"It isn't that simple," Faye said. "But if you actually manage to make progress—"

"According to who? How am I supposed to do that? I'm here because three people are dead! One of them I never got to meet, and now I never will."

Brad exchanged a worried look with Faye.

She wrapped her arm around their daughter. "We know nothing can bring any of them back, and our hearts break for you over that. But you need to try to heal, to move on."

"Why?"

The question jolted Brad. "What do you mean by why?"

"Why heal? Why move on?"

"Because you have a life to live."

"With three people I care about dead and my best friend hating me?"

"You have other friends," Brad said. "Caley and Tyler both stopped by to ask about you."

Hadley wiped her eyes. "They did?"

"Yes. They said a lot of the kids in the play are eager to see you again."

"Not Ellie."

Brad hesitated. "They didn't mention her."

"I'm not going back to school. Ever."

"You don't have to. You're still enrolled in virtual school."

"Why does it matter?"

Faye held Hadley's hand and looked into her eyes. "You can still walk with your class if you graduate from virtual school in time."

"If I don't want to be in class with those people, what makes you think I want to go to that ceremony?"

Brad started to say something, but closed his mouth. It

was a losing battle at this point. She was depressed and grieving, and would likely change her mind by next spring. But it would be a while before she saw clearly again.

The door opened, and the same nurse from earlier came inside. "Time for dinner, Hadley. Say goodbye to your guests."

Hadley stood, showing no emotion. "Bye."

Faye leaped up and embraced her.

Brad hugged her tightly, then put his arm around Faye as they watched their daughter walk away without so much as a glance back at them.

Faye wiped her eyes. "We've got to get her out of this place. She isn't lashing out anymore — we can handle her. I'll drive her to see Dr. Trellis every day if I have to."

Brad kissed her cheek. "Let's look into it. I'll find out what our options are with insurance."

"And I'll call Dr. Fallow to let him know what we're thinking. Hadley can't leave without his approval."

"She'll be home soon," Brad reassured her. "One way or another."

Chapter Three

ZEKE THREW his arms in the air, celebrating yet another win. Not only was he the last player standing, but he'd also found the treasure box in that round. His total XP was skyrocketing, and with it, the number of viewers on his gaming channel.

He stopped the recording, ended the livestream, and turned to his best friend.

Wynn gave him a high-five. "You've gotta put that up on your channel right now! That was epic, dude."

"Can't put it up without editing."

"Who needs editing when you just had a game like that?"

Zeke shook his head. "The videos always need editing."

"Well, this one isn't going to need much. Your views are going to go through the roof after that."

Zeke beamed, even though he didn't want to get his hopes up. "Yeah, but I've had other good games, and they don't always do much."

"This one's going viral. I can feel it in my bones." Wynn pointed to his arm for added effect.

"Maybe." Zeke's heart pounded at the thought. Viral for him at this point would be a few thousand people in the first few days. Some gamers got that as soon as they uploaded. But Zeke had only just started his channel two weeks earlier when he finally got the equipment. It had taken forever before he managed to get to the store when Mom went grocery shopping. He'd bought the gift cards with his cash and ordered everything online.

At almost fifteen, his lifelong dream of having his own gamer channel was finally a reality. It was growing faster than expected. A viral video would really help with momentum.

One day, he would be one of those gamers who made millions each year.

"Are you going to start editing?" Wynn looked at him expectantly.

Zeke's stomach rumbled. "I need a snack."

"Food can wait. This video can't."

"I want to do it right, and I can't do that if I'm hungry."

Wynn scowled. "You're leaving views, likes, and comments on the table."

"You should start your own channel. Then you'll see it isn't as easy as it looks."

"I wish."

"Your dad still won't let you?" Zeke got up and headed for the door.

"Are you kidding? He's certain that someone will kidnap and kill me if my face shows up on a video."

"Maybe you should show him my channel. Or the channels of the millions of other gamers who've never been kidnapped or killed."

"He doesn't care." Wynn deepened his voice. "'As long as you live under *my* roof …'"

"Then make videos at your mom's house. Or while you're here."

He shook his head. "She doesn't want to disagree with him. Says he'll take it to court, and she's sick of judges and lawyers and all the stress. I can't have a channel, period."

"Well, when you do finally start yours, and I'm famous, I'll tell everyone to follow you."

Wynn shrugged. "Let's just start editing your video."

"After food." Zeke opened the door.

A whiff of pot roast hit his nose immediately.

He closed the door. "Grandma already has dinner cooking. She won't let me have a snack now."

Wynn pumped his fist in the air. "Time to start editing — like I said."

"Okay." Zeke sat back down and opened the video editing program. "Check my channel for new comments."

"On it."

The room was so quiet, the only noises were of keyboard tapping and a clicking mouse.

Zeke turned on Aerosmith, and the music helped his concentration.

After a while, Wynn made a grumbling sound.

"You okay?" Zeke didn't pull his attention from the computer screen.

"Looks like you got your first troll."

"What?" Zeke turned to him.

Wynn pointed to his screen. "Right here. JimBob2005."

"Sounds like a troll." Zeke went over to his bed, where Wynn sat with his laptop. "What'd he say?"

"Called you a poser and said some stuff about your sister."

"I've never mentioned Hadley. Is it someone from school?" Zeke shoved him out of the way and read the comment.

JimBob2005: Hey poser, I hear ur sister's a killer. U one 2? Hahaha! Learn 2 play and stop dressing like a freak.

Zeke's heart pounded.

He exchanged a wide-eyed stare with Wynn. "Are people still saying Hadley had something to do with Nate?"

Wynn shrugged.

"That one guy is in jail for kidnapping him. Hadley didn't do anything."

"People are stupid," Wynn offered. "Just delete it. Block him."

"But look — it has almost twenty likes! People agree with him." Anger burned in Zeke's chest.

When would people ever leave his family alone?

"Block the jerk," Wynn said.

"He'll just make a new account."

"Then block that one, too. He'll eventually get bored. Who cares what he says? He's just a troll. Only wants to rattle you."

The troll had managed that much.

"Gimme your password, and I'll delete it."

Zeke shook his head. "I'll do it."

"You know, they say once you get a troll, you've arrived."

"Whatever." Zeke went back to his desk, opened his gamer channel account, and found JimBob's comment. Deleted it. Blocked him.

But it would only be a matter of time before the jerk was back.

"Don't let it get to you," Wynn said. "People don't really think she's a killer."

"Some people obviously do."

"Where is she, by the way? I haven't seen her in a long time."

"How would I know?" Zeke snapped.

"Touché."

Zeke hadn't told his best friend about Hadley being in the mental hospital. Didn't want to, either.

Wynn would think it was hilarious.

He'd never hear the end of it.

Hopefully, she'd be back home soon and her absence would be long forgotten. Zeke had managed to stay quiet about his family's involvement in Nate's death.

Wynn had no clue. It was bad enough that he knew Zeke's dad was an assassin.

Zeke wasn't going to blow any more of his family's secrets.

There were so many of them.

He returned his attention to editing the video.

"You done with that yet?" Wynn asked.

"Not if I want the video to be good." Zeke switched the music to Metallica.

Just as the third song began, Wynn broke his concentration.

"Dude! Look at this!"

Zeke squeezed his eyes shut. "Not another troll."

"No! You won't believe this. Look at your follower count."

"What about it?"

"Just *look*."

It had jumped by more than a hundred.

"How's that possible?" Zeke asked.

Bigger gamers saw those numbers all the time. Not Zeke.

"Someone mentioned you?"

"Maybe."

"You edit, I'll look into it."

Zeke went back to his video, but his mind kept returning to the troll.

Hopefully that was the last he'd hear from him.

Chapter Four

BRAD GLANCED AROUND THE OFFICE. His gaze landed on one of the framed paintings.

Again.

More than anything, he wanted to remove them and find out if there was a safe hiding behind one of them. But the office had to be bugged.

Finding the cameras was not the problem — as soon as Bancroft took them offline, Ralf would know that something was hinky, and Brad would be his number one suspect, despite Bancroft's efforts to make it look like Brad had tried to save Kurt in the official arrest report.

Bancroft's team had been trying to hack into the system that the cameras fed into, so they could insert some kind of loop that would make it look like the office was empty. That way they could search the office for as long as they liked without triggering any alarms.

But Kurt and Ralf had some sort of black market, better-than-military-grade cyber defenses protecting everything. Bancroft's hackers hadn't been able to get in without a brute-force attack, which would have alerted Ralf.

Brad didn't understand any of it.

But he'd played it safe for the last month while he waited for them to quietly crack Ralf's protection — going through the desk, some of the books on the shelves, that type of thing. Didn't do anything he wouldn't in front of Ralf.

But he needed to do more.

It was driving him crazier by the day.

He'd given his login info to Bancroft, and her people.

Maybe what he needed to do was test something. But what? Something that would be big enough for Ralf to show up, but not enough to infuriate him and fire Brad.

It was another fine line to walk.

Knock, knock!

Brad wanted to pull out his hair.

Now he understood why Kurt had always been in a bad mood. People knocked constantly.

Another reason he couldn't start pulling apart the office.

Brad opened the door.

Scott stood on the other side. "Finally got through all the inventory. The knives are in place, and other stuff is in the safe with the money. Anything else I can do?"

Brad relaxed. "You got through that quickly."

"Wasn't hard. What next?"

It was tempting to ask him to help with the office, but he didn't trust Scott *that* much. Not yet, at least. Maybe he'd prove himself to be a confidante later. But for now, Brad had to assume he was loyal to the Bergmanns.

"Are you up for training a new recruit?" Brad asked.

Scott lifted a brow. "How extensive?"

"I'm not sure. Ralf mentioned a new one coming in later today."

"That's all he said?"

"Hung up before I could ask more questions."

"Sounds like him. Yeah, send the recruit my way when he gets here. Or is it a she?"

Brad shrugged. "New recruit. That's all I know."

"Sounds like fun. I'll check on Josh out front." Scott headed for the floor room.

Brad's phone alerted him of a text.

The agent.

She probably wanted a progress report.

Not much to give. As usual.

He locked Kurt's — his — office and headed outside to his car. That was where he spoke to the agent. Didn't trust anywhere else other than his house.

Bancroft answered on the first ring. "What's the news?"

"Nothing."

"No progress?"

"That's what I said."

"What's it going to take?"

Brad thought about it. "Any way you can find out from Kurt if his office is bugged? I *want* to tear the place apart looking for the information we need, but I'm not going to risk Ralf finding out."

"He's out of my hands now. Got all the information out of him that I could, and now he's in prison."

Brad sighed. "Do you have any equipment to detect that sort of thing?"

"Of course I do. What kind of question is that?"

"I need it. That's the only way I'll be able to go through that office — if I know there are no eyes on me."

"You think your boss won't notice his equipment not recording anything?"

"That's not what I said. I simply need a window of time to tear through the place. If they're hiding anything in the building, it has to be in the office. And the last places I have to look are behind the paintings and shelves."

She sighed. "What you need is to get closer to your boss."

"The man is notoriously absent. It isn't unusual to go months without seeing the man. More than a year, even. It's happened."

"Things have changed."

"Right. His new focus is getting his son out prison. He doesn't have to worry about the knife shop with me here."

"All the more reason not to worry about him spying on you."

"The man has cameras on me."

"When do you think they were installed?" she asked.

"What does that have to do with anything?"

"Have they been there since Kurt was in there? Or do you think these cameras were placed after?"

"Your point?" Brad asked.

"Why would anyone put cameras in there when Kurt was there? He wouldn't want them aimed at himself."

"He would've wanted them there in his absence. Or if anything went wrong when someone was in there with him — then he'd have the proof he needed. Makes perfect sense."

The agent paused before responding. "Even if that were the case, do you think Ralf would have access to that? Or know how to use the technology?"

"Of course he would. Kurt worked for *him*. He's the top dog."

"He's also close to ninety."

"Seventy-five," Brad corrected.

"Same difference. I know his type. These guys like to do things old-school. Our technology frustrates them. He doesn't want to take the time to learn it."

"He has people who won't be put off by it."

"You're not going to give up on this, are you?"

"No."

"I can't just hand over the equipment."

Brad drew in a deep breath. "Then bring it in yourself."

"You want me to come into the office?"

"Yes."

"Under what pretense?" she asked.

"Pretend to deliver a package."

"Or …"

Brad grimaced.

Her tone made it sound like he'd hate her idea.

"What?"

"I'll pretend to be interviewing as a new recruit."

"You mean an assassin?"

"That's better than being a delivery driver."

He put her on speaker and rubbed his temples. "That's the only way you'll come in and look for bugs in the office?"

"Yes. It'll be a good show to put on for the cameras — if there are any."

He held back a groan.

"What do you say?" she asked.

"Be here in an hour."

Chapter Five

KNOCK, knock.

The knocking never stopped.

Brad glanced at the time.

Exactly one hour. It might be Bancroft on the other side of the door.

Or it could be the new guy asking some random question again. Probably that. Josh was on break, and Scott was at a doctor's appointment. On a weekday, that left Brad. It seemed like that would be enough of a hindrance for the new guy, but nope. Not him.

Brad drew a deep breath and answered the door just as the knocking began again.

It was Bancroft. Wearing a sharp suit, perfect makeup, and her hair in a tight bun.

He waved her in and closed the door. "You look like a CIA agent."

"I *am* a CIA agent."

Brad laughed loudly. "You're hilarious. You'll fit right in."

She walked past him and looked around, scrutinizing a

painting first — it looked like someone had splashed paint all over it at random. Luna could do better than that. His mom's dog could do better. But given the fact that it was in Kurt's old office, it was probably worth a small fortune.

Bancroft turned to him. "Looks like an original Maggie Oliver."

He gave her a double-take. "Come again?"

"The painting."

"That's your big takeaway?"

She turned to him, turning her nose up slightly. "Are we going to start this interview, or what?"

"I thought you were enjoying the painting."

Bancroft sat and looked at him, clearly expecting him to sit on the other side of the desk.

To conduct an interview.

He sat and chewed on a pen. Then realized it had been Kurt's and spit it out.

She smirked.

"Do you have any experience with assassinations?"

Bancroft tilted her head. "You can't just ask someone that."

"Yes, I can. I'm here to interview you." But it struck him that he had never been in this position before. He'd been on the other side of this desk more than ten years earlier. Could barely remember the day. "Do you?"

"I've been trained to use a gun." She leaned closer. "And I gathered from our previous conversation, you have experience researching people's lives and locations?"

A slow, knowing smile spread across her face. "That I do."

Brad pressed his palms on the table. "Great. Due to your impressive recommendations, I'd like to offer you the job now."

Her eyes widened.

"You don't have to answer right away. In fact, you're more than welcome to stretch your legs and think about it."

"Sounds good." She rose and walked around slowly, not stopping at anything in particular.

Brad rested his forehead on his palms. The whole thing made him feel like an idiot. Though he wasn't sure which was worse — the possibility that Ralf might actually be listening to this farce or the fact that they could be acting without an audience.

"Do you need my decision at any particular time?" Bancroft asked.

"No. Carry on." Brad pulled the laptop closer and typed in the password. Checked his email.

She wandered around slowly, looking. Not touching anything, not saying anything.

It was enough to make him want to scream.

He'd learned to fake patience in his years as an assassin. It was a job requirement. How many hours had he spent waiting for the perfect moment to make his kill?

Then there was parenting and marriage. If *those* hadn't taught him patience, nothing would.

Click, click.

Brad jolted to attention.

The key.

Someone was unlocking the door.

Ralf.

He was the only other person with a key.

Jiggle, jiggle.

Bancroft whipped around, questioning him with her eyes.

"It's Ralf."

She hurried over to the chair and sat again.

Cree-eak.

25

The door opened slowly.

Brad turned to his computer screen and started typing nonsense.

Ralf stepped inside, his bald head tanner than before and his white beard a little fuller. He squinted at Brad first, then at the agent.

Brad pushed his chair back slightly and shut the laptop. He smiled, hoping to cover the fact that his heart pounded like a jackhammer. "Ralf, what a surprise. What brings you in?"

The older man crossed his arms, his muscles bulging through his shirt. He was in better shape than most guys thirty years younger. And twice as intimidating. Even for Brad, a trained assassin.

But he would kill him one day.

Soon.

The silence carried on.

"Can I get you something?" Brad asked. "Last time we spoke, you mentioned needing the—"

"Who is she?" Ralf gestured toward the agent.

"This is Ju—"

Bancroft leaped up and extended her hand toward Ralf. "Name's Jessica Williams. Mr. Morris here just offered me a job."

Ralf cocked a brow. Didn't shake her hand. "Did he?"

Brad nodded. "I did. She's going to be a fantastic addition to the company."

"Meaning?"

"She has plenty of experience, and her references are phenomenal."

"Wonderful news." Ralf's expression remained stoic.

Bancroft gave Brad a curious glance before turning to Ralf. "It's been a pleasure to meet you, but I really must be going." She glanced back at Brad. "I'll see you tomorrow."

"See you then."

The agent studied Ralf as she left, closing the door behind her.

"What's that all about?" Ralf sauntered to the desk, not sitting. "You're hiring someone without running that by me first?"

Brad's throat closed up. He coughed to clear it. "Things have been tough lately with all the—"

"Don't be so nervous, Brad. I'm glad to see you taking some initiative. I don't want to be bothered with small stuff."

Brad's knees turned to rubber. Not many people could bring out these reactions in him, but Ralf Bergmann was no ordinary man.

"You may be wondering why I'm here today."

"I am curious."

Ralf moved aside the chair and sat. Looked expectantly at Brad.

He barely remembered standing. He sat.

"I've been hearing good things from everyone about you."

"You have?" Brad cleared his throat. "I mean, I'm glad to hear it. I've been doing my best."

Ralf nodded, his mouth curved down slightly. "I'd like to invite you to join me and a few of my top executive managers for breakfast this Saturday."

It took Brad a moment to comprehend the words. He was inviting him over to his house. Potentially giving him access to even more sensitive information than could be found here in the office. "Thank you, sir."

Ralf nodded, his expression pinched. "Show up hungry. We'll have plenty of food."

"What time?"

"I'll get you the specifics." Ralf rose. "See you then."

"I wouldn't miss it."

Without a word, Ralf left the office.

Brad leaned back and went over the entire conversation. Though his new boss had looked angry the whole time, his words indicated that Brad was doing a good job. And more importantly, he wanted him to come over.

He'd already been numerous times at Kurt's invitation. That would make it easier to find what he needed for the agent. If only he could bring her there, but Ralf had said it was just a few of his top assassins.

Definitely no new hires would be welcome.

This was good news. Ralf wouldn't have shown up with the invitation if he was spying on Brad here in the office.

Unless it was a test.

He *had* arrived while Bancroft was looking around the office. During their supposed interview.

Was the breakfast what it appeared? Or a trap?

Chapter Six

FAYE TOOK the first bite of sandwich, hungry enough to scarf the whole thing in just a few bites. Her home salon continued to be a success — so much so that she hadn't even had time to take a morning break. This was her first chance to rest.

It was a good thing the agent had found that adult daycare for Dianne, and that she loved being there, because Faye certainly had no time to take care of her mother-in-law while running her business. She was doing the job of several people — receptionist, hair stylist, book-keeper, and janitor — but loving every moment. Though she'd taken to paying Luna each evening to do some of the cleaning. Faye's youngest daughter enjoyed pushing the oversized broom around and had turned finding stray hairs into a game.

It helped her forget how much she missed her big sister.

That reminded Faye she needed to call Dr. Trellis, to see if she'd had a chance to speak with Dr. Fallow yet about Hadley's release.

Ding-dong!

Faye had made it to three bites without a distraction. That couldn't be her next client, could it? If so, the woman was a full half hour early.

No, that was the front door's bell, and she made sure to give clear instructions when scheduling each appointment, telling each person about the dedicated salon door.

She took a quick bite before hurrying down the hall to the front door and peeking out.

The woman standing on the porch was familiar, but Faye couldn't immediately place her. The distortion of the peephole didn't help.

Probably someone from the neighborhood. They'd recently had a bunch of house sales, so there were quite a few new faces, many of which she'd never officially met.

Faye opened the door just as the woman reached for the doorbell again.

"Faye?"

Obviously, they'd met.

"Yes. I'm sorry. I forget your name."

"I'm Paula. We met about a month ago."

Faye tried to remember how they'd met. Maybe she lived two streets over. That seemed vaguely familiar.

"Nate's birth mom," Paula clarified.

The words took the air from Faye's lungs. She recovered quickly. "Right. Paula. I'm so sorry. Can I help you with something?"

She frowned. "Your family was close with the Campbells, right?"

Faye's pulse quickened. "I was friends with Allison, but that was about as far as it went. Our husbands never really hit it off."

"But Nate, he was friends with your older daughter before he disappeared, wasn't he?"

"They talked a little." Faye wanted to lean against the door frame for support, but didn't want to show how shaken she was. "He'd lost Allison and my daughter had suffered a recent loss. But they ran in different circles and didn't spend much time together."

Paula nodded. "Mind if I come in and ask a few more questions?"

Faye glanced at her watch. "I have a client coming by in about twenty minutes."

"I won't take up much of your time. It's just a few questions."

"Okay." Faye's stomach twisted into tight knots. She stepped aside and let the other woman in. "Can I get you some coffee?"

"No. I won't be long."

Faye sat back at her spot at the kitchen table. "Sorry to eat in front of you. I don't have a long lunch break today."

"It's no problem." Paula sniffled as she sat across the table. "As you can guess, I'm dealing with a lot of regret. I never would've given up Nate for adoption if I knew things would end up like this — with him missing and that thug headed for trial for his murder."

Faye nearly choked on her bite of sandwich. "I can't even imagine."

"I was a different person eighteen years ago. It feels like a lifetime, and for Nate it was." Paula drew in a deep breath. "I really thought that I was giving him a better life by not raising him alone. I was only seventeen, and his father — you don't have time for the story. I'm sorry."

"It's okay. Go on."

Paula wiped her eyes. "Hardly a day went by where I didn't think of Nate — though I'd always thought of him as Brandon. I didn't know what name he'd been given. It was always my hope that one day we'd reunite. Obviously, we wouldn't have a typical mother-son relationship, but I pictured we'd have something once he was grown. Maybe his kids would consider me a grandma."

Faye choked. Struggled to free the food.

"Are you okay?"

She nodded, and spit the food into a napkin. "Went down the wrong tube. Continue."

"I'm rambling, and you're on a time crunch. Sorry. It's just that I keep thinking about Nate. Yes, that horrible man is in prison, but they never found my son's body." Paula's voice cracked. "There's still a chance he's out there somewhere. He could have survived. I don't ever want to give up on him."

"No mother would." Faye picked up her plate and took it to the sink before Paula could see the tears in her eyes.

That woman would never get to meet her son.

It broke her heart. And guilt pressed on her chest, from withholding crucial information.

But hold it, she would. Faye had her own child to protect. A living daughter, one who did not need to spend any time in jail.

Hadley was suffering enough without it. The guilt would likely never leave her. Especially since she couldn't talk about it with anyone outside of their family.

That was also why the mental hospital or all the doctors in the world couldn't heal her completely. They could help with the grief of losing her boyfriend, her baby, and even her friend — but they couldn't do a thing about the guilt of accidentally killing Nate.

She and Brad had really screwed up by covering the crime.

The authorities might have seen it for what it was. An accident, provoked by the threats of a grown man. Hadley wouldn't have had the knife on her had Wes not threatened her. Wes was responsible for Nate's death.

Faye realized Paula was talking. She turned back around and returned to the table.

"Your daughter hasn't thought of anywhere Nate might've gone?"

"No, I'm sorry."

Paula pulled out her purse.

Faye froze. Was she going to pull out a weapon?

She held up a cell phone. "Can I get your number? I'd like to talk to you when you have more time, if that's okay with you."

Faye released a breath and rattled off her number.

"I'll get out of your hair." Paula stood. "Thanks for your time."

"No problem. I only wish I could do more to help."

Just as Faye said goodbye to her at the front door, a car pulled up to the curb.

Her next client.

It was going to be one long afternoon.

Chapter Seven

HADLEY THREW THE PAINTBRUSH DOWN.

The face she'd created mocked her. Smirked. Laughed. Taunted.

It was nowhere near his likeness.

She'd been trying to draw Duke, but it looked nothing like him. In fact, it was getting harder to remember what he looked like. Especially without her phone.

Before the accident, she'd spent hours scrolling through photos and rewatching videos of the two of them.

Now she didn't even know where the phone was. It could've been destroyed in the car accident — just like her and Duke's baby.

But the phone didn't matter. Everything was saved on the cloud. Except that she wasn't allowed access to any electronic devices. She had to get out of this stupid hospital. She was the sanest person in the place, and that was including the nurses — they were the real psychos.

She hated it here. Not just because of the nurses or the drugs or the fact that she couldn't look at Duke's beautiful face. It was literally everything. Even the walls bothered her. The soft colors were supposed to be soothing, but she'd have preferred the stereotypical clinical white.

"Why did you stop painting?"

Hadley turned toward the art teacher. "Because it sucks."

She smiled, exposing a ton of crow's feet. "It's lovely."

"It looks nothing like him."

"Who's he?"

"Dead." Hadley crossed her arms. "So's our baby."

The teacher's eyes widened. "I'm so sorry."

"So am I."

"Do you want to try drawing something else?"

"No."

She frowned. "Are you sure?"

"*Yes*."

"You could try making this more to your liking. It really is good."

"It doesn't even look like him."

"Still, you have talent."

"For all the good it does me."

"What if you stopped trying to paint something specific, and just let the painting happen?"

"Just start painting with no end in mind?"

"Your subconscious mind could come up with something you didn't even realize you wanted to draw."

"How would that come out as anything more than scribbles?"

"I'm not saying that couldn't happen, but it's possible that you might make something beautiful."

"Seems unlikely." Hadley turned back to her painting.

It continued to mock her.

She grabbed it. Smashed it on the ground. Stomped on it.

Now a rip covered the two eyes of the non-Duke.

"Much better."

The art teacher frowned.

Hadley carried the paper to the nearest trash bin and stuffed it inside. Breathed a sigh of relief. That was where it belonged.

She marched to the main room where all the crazies hung out. Some were playing kids' board games, others watching a show that looked like it was made in the 60s or 70s, based on the gaudy clothes. Still others were busy by themselves, reading or drawing or talking to themselves. One guy was dancing around, flapping his arms and legs like a chicken, singing what sounded like a ghastly opera.

What the hell was she doing here with these nut jobs? She'd lost some people she cared about, not her mind. The only good thing was that she didn't need to worry about school — virtual or otherwise — or homework. But she would have to make it up at some point.

At least she didn't care about graduating with her class anymore. Seeing any of those people was the last thing she wanted. Her so-called best friend had probably turned everyone against her by this point, even the last few who had been nice to her.

What had been the point of spending so much time working so hard to build her reputation, to become the best actress, to get everyone to love her, when it could all get taken away so quickly? It was there one day and gone the next.

What was the point of anything? Did it matter if she was at school with all those jerks, or if she was here with these people? She could get food thrown at her in either place.

Tears stung, and the lump in her throat grew. It became harder to breathe. She gasped for air, trying to keep the tears at bay.

Her vision grew blurry, her lips wavered.

She burst into a run. Headed for her room.

Not that it was *hers*.

She raced inside. Slammed the door shut behind her. Looked around for something to shove in front of the door. They could lock her in, but she couldn't lock them out. Everything was bolted to the floor, like it could all be used as a weapon.

Except the chairs. She could be trusted with those.

Hadley grabbed one and shoved it under the handle. It took some jockeying, but she got it to fit.

Now they were all locked out.

She was finally truly alone.

Not that she wasn't already. Most of the people who mattered were either dead or had betrayed her. Their faces danced around in her mind. Mocked her worse than the awful painting.

Knock, knock!

It was that horrible nurse. The one she called Ratched. That woman was a psycho. She needed to be locked up in a place like this.

She glowered at Hadley through the small window in the door, yelling something.

Hadley's breathing grew labored.

The nurse pointed and continued knocking.

Images of Duke and Nate swirled between them.

Hadley's tears finally fell loose. Trailed down her face. She struggled to breathe. To gasp in a little air.

It sounded like the nurse was calling her names. Threatening her.

But it was hard to hear over Nate asking why she'd killed him. Over Duke asking why she hadn't saved him. Over the baby crying for her.

Over the kids at school making fun of her. Accusing her of being a murderer.

Hadley ran behind the bed and pressed her back against the wall, sliding down until her butt hit the floor.

Finally out of sight of the nurse.

But she couldn't hide from the faces, the memories.

It was all too much.

How was this place supposed to help anything?

Everything was worse than it ever had been before.

All she wanted was to go home. To her real bedroom.

She'd been just fine before. Or at least better than now.

Definitely better than now.

This was a new low.

She could hardly think over the pounding on the door.

Nurse Ratched was probably going to stuff her full of pills.

Pills that Hadley had quickly learned not to swallow. *Those* made her feel crazy. Loopy and out of it, at best. Nobody seemed to suspect that she'd been flushing them down the toilet.

She needed to come to terms with her new reality. Meds couldn't change that.

Nothing could.

Duke had been murdered. She'd accidentally killed Nate and couldn't tell anyone. But at least someone else was supposed to go down for that. Someone who'd gotten away with much worse. And now Duke's baby was gone, too. Dead as him.

The only thing that gave her any hope was that they were together somewhere. And maybe someday she'd be able to join them.

That thought was sounding better by the moment.

Especially with the actual crazy woman outside her door who wouldn't stop with the pounding and hollering.

Hadley looked around for something she could use to stop all the madness.

But the room was about as dangerous as a padded room.

They'd thought of everything ahead of time.

She'd probably been on suicide watch since day one.

The irony was she hadn't been thinking along those lines at all then.

Now she was.

The only thing that sounded good was joining Duke and their baby.

It was the only thing that made any sense.

The one thing she wanted.

Somehow, she'd make it happen.

Chapter Eight

BRAD PACED the office for what had to be the five-hundredth time, his mind racing. Either Ralf didn't know that Brad knew he was the one to call the hit on his dad's life, or he was eager to take Brad out.

This breakfast could either be Brad's chance at revenge, or his final meal before Ralf executed him.

Either way, Brad was up for the challenge.

He'd wanted to avenge his dad's death for thirty years.

There wasn't much time to prepare for the big event. Not that it mattered. He'd been thinking about this for so long. Brad always got his targets. Even when he ran into obstacles. When others wanted to kill him.

He knew how to get the job done.

This would be trickier than the typical hit, however. It would be in Ralf's home. The man had been in the business longer than Brad had been alive. And the house would be full of the best assassins, all who worked for Ralf Bergmann.

It would be Brad's final target. The most dangerous.

Then he would be done. Could wash his hands of everything. Walk away from it all.

What would he do without the only career he knew anymore? Go back to real estate?

He laughed at the thought. The market was far better now than when it had crashed after the golden heyday.

No, he wasn't going back to that life. Showing people houses would be a drag after such an exciting career.

Knock, knock.

He would have plenty of time to figure out what to do with the rest of his life. For now, he needed to plot Ralf's demise.

And before he did that, he needed to answer the door.

Scott stood on the other side. "Well?"

"Well, what?" Brad stepped aside to let the other assassin in.

"Are you going?"

Brad nodded.

"What do you make of it?" Scott leaned against a wall.

"Pretty sure it has something to do with Kurt's arrest." Brad sat behind the desk.

"You don't think he wants us to break him out of prison?"

"That would be crazy."

"Wouldn't be out of the realm of possibility."

"Maybe he wants something else."

"Like what?" Scott took the seat on the other side of the desk.

"Got me."

"You're not curious?"

"Of course I am. But I don't have enough information to do more than speculate wildly."

"Ralf needs Kurt to take over the empire he's spent a

lifetime building," Scott said. "He's the only one he's trained for the job."

"That we know of."

Scott lifted a brow. "You think he has someone else ready?"

"Ralf is too crafty to limit himself to a single end, and he hasn't gotten where he is by not preparing for things to go wrong."

"That's an angle I hadn't considered, but I think you're right. You've probably spent more time with Ralf than the rest of us."

"He's been absent as usual, for the most part. I'm surprised he's been so hands-off."

Scott leaned closer. Spoke in a whisper. "I have a theory about that, too."

"What?"

He looked around. "Let's talk somewhere else. Lunch break?"

Brad's heart raced.

Scott didn't trust the Bergmanns either?

Brad started to agree, but his phone rang.

The agent. She would want to know what Ralf had spoken to him about.

They could talk while he drove to the restaurant.

He glanced back at Scott. "Now would be a great time."

"Perfect. I've been dying to try that new Indian place near the bowling alley. Meet there in twenty?"

Brad checked the time. "Sounds like a plan."

As Scott saw himself out, the phone rang again.

Brad sent Bancroft a quick text, letting her know he'd call back in a few minutes. He gathered a few things, locked the office, then let the guys working the store know he would be out.

Once in his car, he called the agent and put the phone on speaker before heading out.

Scott's car was already gone.

"What did Bergmann want?" Agent Bancroft answered.

"He's putting together a breakfast at his house on Saturday for his top assassins."

"That sounds promising."

"Except that I have no idea what he wants to discuss."

"It is curious that he arrived while I was there."

"Exactly."

"You're going to take advantage of the time to look for what I need." It wasn't a question.

"That's the plan." After killing the old man, of course.

"What's the hesitation?"

"Hesitation?"

"Don't play dumb with me," she snapped. "What are you holding back?"

She was on to him. "Nothing."

"Brad." Her tone was like that of an annoyed teacher who held his grade in the balance. But she held much more than that.

He took a deep breath. Could *not* let her know he wanted to kill the man. "It's just going to take some careful planning. I'm on my way to have lunch with another assassin who's going to be there."

"He doesn't know about our working relationship, does he?"

"Nobody does."

"Other than your wife and daughter."

"That goes without saying."

"And how is Hadley?"

Brad clenched his jaw. "Still in the mental hospital — thanks to her job at the car wash."

"It was your boss who sent that man after her."

"You should've protected her!"

"We've been over this."

"Doesn't change the fact that you didn't do enough. My daughter should be home with her family. Not in that sterile hospital room. And by sterile, I mean being cared for by people who don't know her. She's just another crazy to them. I can see it in their eyes."

The agent took a deep breath on the other end of the line, making a static noise over the phone's speaker. "I told you, my guy protected her. It would've gone a lot worse without his assistance."

"Hadley said she was the only other car on the road other than the one trying to kill her."

"Then she didn't see my guy. But he was there, and it *would* have been a lot worse without him. Notice that she survived. The perpetrator was the one who had the collision. Not Hadley."

Anger pulsed through him. It was a good thing Bancroft was on the other side of a phone line.

"Do you want me to pull some strings to get her out of there?"

"You can do that?" Brad exclaimed. "That would have been useful information."

"You *know* I can pull strings."

"With the police."

"And plenty of other agencies."

Now he wanted to hit something more than before.

"You still there?" she asked.

"Yes."

"Do you want me to speak with her doctor? What's his name?"

Brad squeezed the steering wheel as he pulled up to a

stoplight. "Dr. Fallow. He's the one at the hospital. Her normal doctor is Dr. Trellis. She's our family therapist."

"I'll see what I can do."

"I thought you said you can pull strings."

"Yes, but that doesn't mean you can bring her home tonight. This may require a workaround or two that could take some finagling. I have far more contacts with the prison system than I do psychiatric hospitals."

"Maybe you can use your guy who protected my daughter so well." Brad was tempted to end the call, but didn't dare.

Not when the agent held the power to give or take immunity from both him and Hadley.

"Keep your phone on. I'll be in contact."

"I'll be waiting."

The call ended.

With any luck, the agent could get Hadley out as quickly as she'd managed to get Brad out of the holding cell at the police department.

He pulled into the parking lot of the bowling alley and up to the new building which housed the Indian restaurant and an old-style barber shop, complete with the painted red-and-white pole.

Just as he opened his car door, the phone rang.

"That was fast."

He looked at the screen.

It wasn't Bancroft.

The front desk of the mental institution.

No call from them was good news.

His stomach twisted as he accepted the call.

Chapter Nine

BRAD ENDED the call and rubbed his temples. He'd been right. The call brought bad news. Not horrible, not the worst, but not what he'd wanted to hear.

Hadley had locked herself in her room at the facility, and it had taken the janitor removing the door hinges so the staff could get to her.

She was currently sedated.

His heart broke for her. She didn't deserve this. It needed to end.

Now.

This would be the last call he received informing him of his daughter being sedated.

And he wasn't waiting for Agent Bancroft to pull her strings.

Brad would deal with it himself. Immediately.

He looked up at the building in front of him — the Indian restaurant. That reminded him of his meeting with Scott. The meeting would have to be postponed.

Brad called Scott and took deep breaths, trying to calm

himself. He needed to think straight. Talk to Faye. What-ever action they took, they both needed to be on board.

"Hey, Brad," Scott answered. "Everything okay?"

"No. I have some family stuff to deal with. I have to give you a rain check. Also, can you keep an eye on things at BlueBlade? I'm not sure I'll be able to make it back in this afternoon."

"Sure, whatever you need. Is it anything I can help with?"

"No, but I appreciate the offer. If you can handle the store, that would be a huge help."

"I'm on it. Mind if I grab a bite first?"

"That's fine. And thanks, Scott."

"Don't mention it. If everything is okay with your family by tomorrow, let's meet for lunch then. I still want to talk about this."

"Sounds great." Brad hung up, then called Faye on speaker.

"Did you hear about Hadley?" she answered.

At least he wouldn't have to fill her in on the details. "Yes. They called you too, I take it."

"Just got off the phone with the receptionist."

"We're getting her out of there."

"How? She wasn't a voluntary admission. We have to get the doctor's permission."

"Then we'll get it. I'm on my way home."

"Now?" Faye exclaimed.

"Yes. I told you, we're getting her out. Today."

"What's your plan?"

"I'm picking you up, then we're going to demand Dr. Fallow's attention."

"But that's over an hour's drive."

"My car has plenty of gas."

"But what about my next client? Or Luna? Someone needs to be here when she gets off the school bus. And somebody has to pick up your mom. The adult daycare doesn't stay open all night."

Brad wanted to stop the car and kick something. "How long will your next appointment take?"

"Half hour, tops. But this is a new client and I don't want to cancel on her."

"Our daughter needs us."

"I realize that," she snapped. "But this is also not the first time she's been sedated. She'll still probably be sedated when we get there."

"I'm going to pick up my mom from the daycare and bring her home. She'll be fine watching Luna for a little while. Zeke will also be home from school before too long. Then we get Hadley."

"Okay." A rustling noise sounded on her end of the line. "It looks like my client is here a little early. I should be able to leave sooner than expected."

"Great. I'll be home soon."

They said their goodbyes and ended the call.

Brad changed his direction to pick up his mom, and called the agent.

"You're impatient," she answered.

"Change of plans."

"What?" If a tone of voice could kill, Brad would be dead on the spot.

"Those nurses have sedated my daughter *again*. I'm bringing her home tonight."

"I haven't even—"

"I'm not waiting for anyone. If I have to break her out myself, then that's what I'm doing."

"Let me handle it."

He pulled into the parking lot and squealed into a spot. "And how long will that take?"

"More than a few minutes."

"That doesn't tell me anything."

"I got you out of that holding cell, didn't I? And I found someone to take the fall for what she did. I think I've earned the right to your trust."

Brad clenched his fists. "Can you get her out tonight?"

"Can you promise me you'll get the information I need from your boss this weekend?"

"I'll do whatever it takes."

"Great. Then give me time to see what I can do about your daughter, Mr. Morris."

He bit back an annoyed retort. "Okay. Thank you."

As soon as the call ended, he went inside to pick up his mom.

She was playing cards with a man in a Hawaiian shirt and a bright smile. And she was smiling wider than he'd seen in a long time.

Brad was glad to see her in good spirits, but eyed the man with suspicion. They just seemed to be enjoying a game together. He went over to one of the staff members. "Tell me about that guy playing cards with my mom."

"Richard?" she asked. "He's a real sweetheart. Been coming in almost every day for a few weeks now."

"Coming in?" That seemed like an odd word choice.

"Unlike most of the others here, he checks himself in and out. Comes for the company, not because he needs anyone watching him."

"Does that happen often?" Brad asked. "I mean, do others come in for that reason?"

"Once in a while." She glanced over at Richard. "His wife passed away a few months ago, and he's pretty lonely.

From what he's told me, she had dementia, and he cared for her until the end. Now he has nobody."

"No kids?"

She shrugged. "Not that I'm aware of. Like I said, he's a good guy."

Brad nodded, and turned his attention back to Richard.

"Has he been spending much time with my mom?" Brad asked.

"Yeah. Your mom is one of the more coherent ones, and they have a lot of fun playing cards together. Oh, I need to help Gladys." She hurried over to one of the elderly ladies.

Brad checked the time. Faye should be wrapping up with her client any minute, so he needed to get back home.

He went over to the table and introduced himself to Richard, who gave him a firm handshake and a smile that reached his eyes.

"It's pleasure to meet you. Your mom is giving me a run for my money at pinochle."

"You're gambling?" Brad exclaimed.

Richard laughed. "Good one. No, this is all in good fun."

Brad turned to his mom. "I'm glad you're making friends. We need to get home, though. Faye and I have something to take care of, and we need you to watch Luna, if you're feeling up to it."

She beamed. "I'd never turn down time with my grandkids."

"I wouldn't either." Richard rose and helped her out of her chair. "I hope you'll be back tomorrow, and we can finish our game then."

"I'm here every weekday."

"Great."

Their gazes lingered for a moment before Brad's mom turned back to him. "Is everything okay? Where do you and Faye need to go?"

He put his hand on her shoulder and guided her toward the door. "Nothing for you to worry about, Mom."

"What is it? You don't have to hide things from me."

If only she knew.

"We're trying to bring Hadley home. There are a lot of … complications."

"Is she doing better? I've been so worried about her."

"She misses everyone."

"Such a shame, having to be institutionalized like that, especially at her age. She has so much going for her."

"Yes, she does." Brad helped her into the car before getting into his side and starting the engine.

"When she gets back, I'll help out however I can. Don't be afraid to ask. I'm getting stronger every day. In fact, I think I'll be ready to go back home soon."

Brad turned to her, his pulse speeding up. "You want to move back to your house?"

"Yes. I'm doing much better, you have to admit."

"Let's wait to see how you do once you get your casts removed."

"I'll finally be able to maneuver the stairs again."

"I don't know about that."

"You'll see. Both my energy and mental clarity have been improving every day — even more since Richard and I have been playing cards together. I'd like to see him outside of the daycare."

"What?" Brad exclaimed.

"We could have him over for dinner."

"I'm not sure what to think about him." Brad clenched the steering wheel.

"He's a stand-up man."

"What does that mean?"

"It means you have nothing to worry about, *son*."

His mom was starting to feel like a third teenager.

He would need to get Richard's last name and look into him.

Chapter Ten

SOMETHING HIT the back of Zeke's head. Felt like wadded paper.

He whipped around, unable to tell who threw it in the busy hallway. Plenty of kids were laughing, but nobody was looking at him.

"Jerk," he muttered.

"What?" Wynn asked.

"Nothing."

Something else hit him. This time it was harder, like an eraser. Next time, it could be something that could cause damage.

He spun around, holding up his fists. "Who threw that?"

Nobody paid him any attention.

Wynn grabbed his shoulder. "Come on. Let's just get to the bus."

Zeke narrowed his eyes and scanned the throng of middle schoolers. "Too afraid to admit you threw it? Scared of me?"

"Come *on*." Wynn pulled him toward the doors.

Zeke didn't budge. "Face me like a man!"

A couple girls from drill team giggled, pointing at him.

His face heated, but he didn't care. He wasn't going to cower from bullies.

The bullies, however, weren't showing their faces.

Typical.

Zeke finally followed Wynn outside to the bus lines.

Nothing else hit the back of his head.

"You gotta just ignore them," Wynn said.

"No. That only encourages them. If they have something they want to say to me, they can say it to my face. Then they can deal with my fists."

Wynn sighed. "You don't want to get into a fight."

"No, *you* don't. I'm ready to show them what I'm made of."

"Your funeral."

"I'm not afraid of them."

Wynn studied him. "What's gotten into you lately?"

"I'm sick of getting picked on. Who cares if my hair is unruly? Or that I like 80s stuff? Doesn't give them permission to treat me like I don't matter."

"Ignoring them has worked fine all this time."

"It hasn't. And it isn't going away. Not with some people still saying crap about Hadley being involved with Nate's disappearance."

They sat in their usual seat near the middle of the bus.

Wynn pulled out his sci-fi novel and stuck his nose in it.

Zeke glanced at the kids still piling onto the bus.

A pretty brunette smiled and waved him as she passed. "Hey, gamer."

His mouth fell open.

But he didn't have time to think about the girl.

Lance, the captain of the wrestling team, got on the bus, laughing with his teammates. His gaze locked on

Zeke's. Something about the way he glowered at him told Zeke that he'd been the one throwing things at him in the hallway.

As Lance passed, Zeke stuck out his foot, making contact with his ankle.

The wrestler lost his balance, his eyes widening and his arms flailing. Crashed into the snobby cheerleader in front of him.

She fell onto the lap of a kid with greasy hair who always smelled like an old laundry basket. She shrieked and leaped up.

Lance crashed onto the floor, skidding. When he sat up, an angry red mark ran up the side of his face, stopping just below his eye. He looked around, cracking his knuckles.

"You shouldn't have done that."

"No, *he* should've left me alone."

Lance marched toward Zeke, his face reddening.

"Get to your seats!" the bus driver ordered.

Lance's nostrils flared as he glared at Zeke. "You're gonna pay, loser."

"Now," the driver demanded.

Wynn leaned closer. "He's going to pummel you."

"I'd like to see him try."

"Are you crazy? He's captain of the wrestling team."

"My point exactly."

"You're not making any sense."

"If he lays a hand on me, he'll get in trouble. Probably have to sit out the next game. Think he wants that? Me, on the other hand, I have nothing to lose. By the time we get off the bus, he'll have figured that out and won't touch me."

"I hope you're right."

Zeke glanced back. "I am."

"What if he sends a friend after you? Someone who also has nothing to lose?"

"Then I'll fight him. I'd rather get beaten up and get it over with than be harassed all the time."

Wynn shook his head and turned back to his book.

Zeke pulled out his phone, covering it with his bag since they weren't supposed to have them out on the bus. He'd been sneaking peeks at his gaming channel all day. The views, likes, and comments were increasing at a crazy rate.

And there were even more now.

"Put that away before you get us both in trouble." Wynn shoved him.

"Look. I have fifty more likes."

Wynn turned away. "Show me when we get to your room. If I get in any trouble at all, I can't play in that tournament this weekend. My dad's mad at me because he thinks I've been rude to his girlfriend."

"Fine." Zeke started to put it away, but then a comment caught his attention because it had two lines in all-caps. The virtual equivalent to yelling.

He glanced around, making sure nobody was paying him any attention — not that anyone ever did, unless it was to make fun of him or throw things at him — and he read the comment. His heart pounded faster with each word he read.

JimBob was back, this time with a different set of numbers in his username.

Wynn poked him. "I thought you were gonna put that away."

Zeke ignored him, focusing on the comment. Or at least trying. It was long and convoluted with the two lines of all-caps. However, it was the last line that made his blood run cold.

JimBob1912: I no who the real assassin is. It isn't ur character. Who's ur daddy?

The troll knew about his dad's profession.

How? Was he also an assassin?

Or had Wynn gone back on his word and told someone?

Maybe his friend was the troll. Jealous of Zeke's success.

Wynn wasn't allowed to start a gaming channel.

Could his best friend have turned on him?

Or was this something far more dangerous?

Chapter Eleven

BRAD CHECKED HIS PHONE AGAIN. No messages or calls from Bancroft.

It was a good thing he'd listened to his gut and insisted on speaking with the doctor. Luckily, their family psychologist Dr. Trellis had agreed to squeeze them in between clients.

Faye put down the magazine she hadn't been reading. "How much longer?"

He glanced at the time. "Should be a few minutes."

"That's what you said a few minutes ago."

"We're fortunate she got us in at all."

"I suppose you're right." She looked at her phone. "I wish Dr. Fallow would call back."

"He knows we want to bring Hadley home. Maybe he's working on that as we speak."

She tapped the armrest. "I hope you're right."

He did, too.

Brad's mind bounced back and forth between worrying about his daughter and his mother. He should've gotten more information about Richard before leaving the daycare center. Now he'd have to wait until morning. He wanted to look up the man's record now.

His mom wasn't rich, so that couldn't be his angle. She had nothing to offer anyone financially.

Maybe Richard was one of those men who liked weak women — someone to control. His mom definitely gave off those vibes with her casts and scars from the stitches. Granted, she was growing stronger by the day, both in mind and body.

Or he could have been sent by Ralf, as insurance. Or leverage. Or both.

Kurt knew about the daycare and could've easily mentioned it to Ralf.

He wished he'd thought to ask Bancroft if the man was a plant, to keep Brad's mother safe. She'd been the one to get his mom into the adult daycare in the first place, making it sound like it had been an ordeal to find an opening. And yet, here was Richard who didn't even need assistance. Just wanted company, and coincidentally enough, picked Brad's mom.

Seemed odd that Bancroft wouldn't mention it to Brad, but she also said nothing about anyone else watching the family.

Any of the above were valid options. Or Richard could just be a nice guy, like everyone seemed to think.

Brad doubted he could be that lucky. Next time he spoke with Bancroft, he was going to ask about that — after he found out what was going on with Hadley. Bringing her home was the first priority. The daycare was safe, with all the workers and plenty of cameras, and Richard couldn't legally leave with her. Only Brad or Faye could sign her out.

Dr. Trellis's door opened, and the psychologist escorted the departing couple out.

"Come on in, you two." She waved Brad and Faye in. "I wish I had more time to give you, but it sounded urgent. Let's see what we can do in ten minutes."

"Thank you." Faye smiled appreciatively.

Brad wrung his hands together. Ten minutes likely would barely scratch the surface. But he'd wait the fifty minutes while she spoke with her next client if he needed to. Whatever it would take to get her to agree to let Hadley come home.

The doctor flipped through some notes. "It looks like Hadley was sedated again today after locking herself in her room."

"Is that normal?" Brad demanded. "They keep sedating her. It seems like they could try harder to work with her. How does locking herself in put anyone else at risk?"

"The nurse believed she posed a threat to herself."

Brad didn't bother holding back an eyeroll. "That's probably the same woman that Hadley calls Ratched. Not that I blame her. The woman is awful."

Dr. Trellis tilted her head. "Do you believe she doesn't have Hadley's best interests in mind?"

"That's the feeling I get," Faye said.

"And you?" Dr. Trellis asked Brad.

"Yes."

"Do you have evidence of this, or just feelings? I can't do much about feelings, but if you have actual proof, I can."

He and Faye both shook their heads.

"I can't do anything about it, then."

"We just want to bring her home," Faye said. "Can you sign off on that?"

Dr. Trellis blinked a few times. "You want to bring her home?"

"They're not helping her, not listening. Just sedating her," Brad said. "The meds they have her on aren't helping. And that place is so sterile. What she needs is fresh air, sunshine, and the love of her family. She isn't getting any of that there. We've given it plenty of time, and it isn't working. Time for something else."

She made notes on one of the pages. "I'll have to speak with Dr. Fallow."

Faye leaned forward. "I'll drive Hadley to see him every day, if that's what it'll take. I don't care about the distance."

"Or she can speak with me."

"You'd do that?" Faye exclaimed.

"Of course. But like I said, I need to speak with Dr. Fallow. He's the one who's seen her every day for the last few weeks."

Brad reached for Faye's hand. "Are you going to recommend Hadley's release?"

"It will depend on what he has to say, but it does sound like it would be in her best interest to be at home."

Relief flooded him, and he leaned back in the chair.

Dr. Trellis looked up at the wall clock. "I should have time to call him quickly before my next client, unless you have more questions."

"No." Brad leaped up and helped Faye to her feet. "Go ahead and call him. We'll get out of your hair."

Brad and Faye saw themselves out as Dr. Trellis dialed her phone.

Faye closed the door behind them. "Let's hope Dr. Fallow agrees that Hadley would be better off at home."

Brad squeezed her hand. "Let's get home and have some dinner. We might have a long night ahead of us."

Faye threw her arms around him. "I hope so."

"So do I."

Chapter Twelve

HADLEY BLINKED A FEW TIMES. Everything was white. Quiet.

Peaceful.

Was she in Heaven?

She tried to sit up. Was yanked back down. Restraints gripped her wrists. She pulled on her legs. But her ankles were strapped down as well.

This was certainly not Heaven. The opposite, if anything.

Hadley fought against the belts. The leather dug into her skin.

That made her all the more resolute. She struggled and strained, ignoring the pain.

Finally, she cried out.

The door opened. Footsteps neared.

Ratched appeared in her periphery. "You're going to injure yourself."

"Let me out!"

"Not after the stunt you pulled earlier."

"I didn't hurt anyone." She struggled all the more.

The nurse smirked. "You're only hurting yourself."

Hadley spat on her. It wasn't like they could make her situation worse than it already was.

Ratched grabbed her face and squeezed. "You want me to tighten those straps?"

"I want to go home!"

"Fat chance, brat."

Hadley tried to build enough saliva to spit again, but the nurse moved out of the way.

The leather around her right wrist tightened.

"You're hurting me!"

"Nobody can hear you. These rooms are soundproof so you crazies can't scare each other with your hollering."

"I'm not crazy!"

"You're the worst of the bunch. I'd know. I have to deal with the whole lot of you."

Hadley screamed so loud it made her throat burn.

The strap around her other wrist tightened. Dug into the skin. Cut into the flesh. Pain shot up her arm, and her hands began to feel numb.

She thrashed harder, crying out.

"Feel like more of the same on your ankles?" the nurse taunted.

The door opened, and the evil nurse backed away from Hadley.

"Help me!" Tears ran down Hadley's face.

"What's going on?"

That was Dr. Fallow's voice.

Relief washed through Hadley. Then worry.

What if he sided with the nurse?

The strap around her right hand loosened. Then her left.

Dr. Fallow appeared over her, concern in his eyes. "Are you okay?"

"I think so." Aside from the throbbing bruises that were already starting to form on her wrists.

The doctor set her free from the ankle restraints before ordering the nurse out of the room and calling for assistance.

One of the nice nurses appeared and began speaking with the doctor in low tones.

Hadley sat up, dizziness washing over her for a moment, and rubbed her raw ankles with hands that were still half-numb. If no one had heard her scream, the evil nurse would've left her like that. Her hands could have been damaged if the circulation was cut for long enough.

Maybe she would've lost them.

The new nurse came over and took care of Hadley's wrists while Dr. Fallow spoke. His words ran together and made no sense. Until he said something about going home. Or at least that was what it sounded like.

"Did you say I can go home?"

He nodded, his mouth curving down as he glanced at her bruises. "Why did she tighten your restraints like that?"

"Because she likes torturing people!"

Dr. Fallow's brows furrowed. "Has Nurse Peterson been doing this for a while? I haven't seen anything like this."

Hadley ran her fingers over the new bandage. "She's never hurt me like this before."

"But you think she enjoys torture?" He didn't sound like he doubted her. Maybe he'd believe her.

She squirmed. "She makes a lot of threats. Calls me names."

His mouth formed a straight line. "Is this true?"

Hadley nodded.

"This shouldn't be." He turned to the nice nurse, and they spoke quietly before he turned back to Hadley. "Nurse

Sanchez is going to help you get ready for your parents' arrival while I speak with some of the other patients about this. Is there anything else you want to tell me about Nurse Peterson before I go?"

Hadley started to say something, but the evil woman appeared in the doorway. She shook her head.

Dr. Fallow turned around, his body tensed. "Excuse me."

He left the room, and sharp tones sounded in the hallway.

Nurse Sanchez gave Hadley a kind smile. "Can I get you anything? Some water? Pain medication for the cuts?"

Hadley rubbed her temples. She had a headache. "Do I really get to go home?"

"Yes, sweetie. From what I understand, your parents are on their way now."

The room seemed to brighten. Her heart pounded at the thought of going home. She was really leaving this horrible place.

"We should get you ready," the nurse added. "Do you want something for your head?"

Hadley nodded and slid her feet over to the floor. Her ankles burned, but held her weight. "Do I get to keep my artwork?"

Not all of them sucked like the one she'd made today.

"I can send for them. Is there anything else?"

Hadley thought about it. "No."

"What about your belongings?"

"The only things I came with were my clothes, but they were ruined." Her stomach lurched at the thought of all the blood on her pants. Not from the car chase, but from losing the baby.

A doctor at the hospital said she'd have lost the baby

eventually anyway. Something wrong with the placenta. Most of what she'd said sounded like Greek.

It still didn't make her feel any better. The baby had been part of Duke, part of both of them.

All of her dreams and hopes were now dead.

Nurse Sanchez said something and hurried out of the room.

Hadley walked around the room, cringing at her burning, sore ankles. Her wrists were about the same, but she didn't have to put any pressure on those.

The nurse reappeared with two bags. She held up one. "Your shirt, bra, socks, and jacket are wearable, and they've been laundered." She raised the other bag. "This one has new pants and underwear. Your shoes are in the closet. Why don't you get dressed? Your parents will be here soon."

Hadley took the bags. "Thanks."

"If you need anything else, let me know. I'll be back with some ibuprofen." She left the room.

The room spun around Hadley. She was really going home?

It hardly seemed possible.

She dumped the contents of the bags onto the bed and got dressed. The jeans were loose and stiff, but they were better than nothing. Especially considering she'd arrived in a hospital gown and bathrobe.

Knock, knock.

Hadley tensed, expecting Ratched, but then realized Dr. Fallow wouldn't send her back to the room. Plus, she wouldn't knock.

"Come in!"

The door opened.

Mom and Dad walked in.

The lump in her throat exploded, and she dissolved

into tears. She'd never been so happy to see them. She raced over and threw her arms around both of them, sobbing.

They surrounded her, which normally would've been suffocating, but now she couldn't ask for anything more.

"Am I really going home?"

Dad stepped back, his eyes shining and a slow smile spreading across his face. "Yes, and everyone is excited to see you. Even Zeke."

Hadley grinned. "Is Grandma still staying with us?"

Mom kissed her cheek. "She is, though she's talking about wanting to return home soon. Her stitches have been removed, and the casts are coming off soon."

"And your salon?" Hadley asked. It felt like she'd been away for years.

"It's off to a great start."

"I'm so happy for you." And she really was.

Dad patted her shoulder. "You ready to go? We have a long drive ahead of us."

"We can stop off and get mochas," Mom said.

Hadley looked out the window, where it was dark outside. "This late?"

"You're coming home — you can have as much caffeine as you want."

Her heart warmed.

Maybe things were finally starting to turn around.

Chapter Thirteen

FAYE CLOSED Hadley's door and tiptoed downstairs. Even with the flavored latte, Hadley had fallen asleep in the car the night before and barely woken long enough to hug everyone before collapsing into bed. Now it was almost lunchtime, and she was still sleeping.

It hurt Faye's heart to think about what she'd gone through in the mental facility. Clearly, it had exhausted her. Unless it was the trauma. Or maybe it was the meds.

Hadley said she hadn't been taking them, but Faye didn't want to risk any negative side effects, so she insisted that her daughter wean off them like Dr. Fallow instructed.

But at least she was home. Faye could check on her any time she wanted. There were no receptionists, nurses, or doctors standing between her and her child any longer.

Exactly the way it should be.

Faye glanced at the time. Ten minutes before her next client. Just enough time to grab a quick snack. Maybe an extra cup of coffee. After the long night, she was wiped out. She'd checked on Hadley at least half a dozen times, because she could.

She made herself another cuppa while warming up a small plate of leftovers in the microwave.

Just as she was finishing the last bite, the buzzer from the salon entrance sounded. She left the plate on the table and hurried to her work space.

She opened the door, surprised to see a six-foot-some-thing man with a full beard and tattoos covering his neck standing there. Not one to make assumptions or judgments, she smiled. "Kirstin?"

"No. My girlfriend couldn't make her appointment, so I came in her place. I'm Jason." He extended his hand, showing more colorful designs.

She shook his hand. "Pleasure to meet you, Jason. I'm Faye. What can I do for you today?"

"Buzz cut. You can do that?"

"No problem. You want a wash first?"

"Is that normal? My barber usually just starts clipping."

"I can do that, too. Whatever you feel comfortable with is fine by me."

He sat in the chair. "Just washed it this morning. Didn't put any gel or anything in it."

"Sounds good." She found a pair of clippers and looked through the different guards. "How short do you want it?"

"Short as you can without making me bald."

She found the right guard and got to work. Asked a few questions, trying to start a conversation. Barely got one-word responses from him, hardly more than a grunt. Some clients were quieter than others, but this guy took the cake. Mostly just looked around. Almost seemed to be trying to look into the main part of the house through the mirror.

But that was crazy.

Or was it?

Faye had never met Kirstin. She was a new client. And come to think of it, she'd made her appointment through the new online form.

Jason himself could've set the appointment, and his girlfriend might not exist.

Though her pulse was now drumming in her ears, she forced herself to focus. The last thing she needed was a repeat of her last client at the big salon — the one she'd messed up on before quitting on the spot.

Now she was alone with this burly guy who might have ulterior motives. Hadley was sleeping upstairs, could come down at any moment.

She glanced around for anything that might be used as a weapon. There were plenty of items, including the clippers in her hand — the razor and the cord would both work. But her phone was out of reach, and that made her even more nervous.

From now on, she'd keep it in her pocket when with a client. Or at least when she was with a new one. Or with a man. She needed to be safe.

Maybe she could have Brad rig up something that attached to the security system.

But for now she was on her own.

She was almost done, thank goodness. After making a few final touches, she stepped away, forced a smile, and handed him a mirror, spinning him so he could look at the back. "How does that look?"

"Better than my barber does." He nodded in approval before handing her the mirror. "Maybe I'll have to switch to you."

"I'm glad you like it." She replaced the mirror on the counter and slid her phone into her back jeans pocket.

"How much do I owe you? Or did Kirstin pay online?"

"She paid for the cut." Or Jason did, and was

pretending ignorance. "Whether you want to give a tip is up to you."

"Definitely." He pulled out his wallet and handed her a ten. "I hope that's sufficient."

"It's perfect. Thanks so much, Jason."

"Have a good afternoon." He headed for the door.

"You too."

Faye breathed a sigh of relief as soon as he closed the door behind him. Maybe she'd read too much into his silence. She hated that she had to be this paranoid.

She slipped on gloves, then placed the bill into an envelope and marked it with his name. Just in case she needed his fingerprints later. Then she wrote out a quick description of his appearance. With everything else going on, there wasn't any room for mistakes.

Her next two clients came and went without a hitch; both were quick haircuts. By the time the last one left, Faye had relaxed a little. She would still talk to Brad about connecting the security system into the salon.

Lunchtime. Her stomach rumbled for an actual meal.

Hadley was still sleeping, so Faye warmed herself a full plate of leftovers. After eating, she still had a solid half hour before her first afternoon appointment.

It was a cloudless day, so she went to the front yard and pulled some weeds from around the tulips. The sun warmed her back and the work was refreshing.

"Faye?"

She glanced up.

Paula stood at the edge of the sidewalk and driveway.

Nate's birth mom. What did she want?

Faye rose and dusted her knees. "Hi, Paula."

"I'm not disturbing you, am I?"

Of course she was. But Faye smiled. "Can I help you with something?"

The other woman frowned. "I'm still looking for clues that will lead to Nate."

"I wish I could help you."

"Have you had a chance to talk to your teenagers?"

"They don't know anything. Neither have seen or heard from him since he disappeared."

"Would you and your husband allow me to speak with your daughter? I can't shake the feeling that talking with her might reveal something."

Faye's stomach knotted. It was time to work another angle. She stepped closer to the desperate mother. "Can I level with you? Mom to mom?"

Paula's eyes widened. "Please do."

Faye leaned against the maple tree. "Hadley has been going through an extremely rough time. Nate is one of three people that she's lost this year."

"I thought you said Hadley and Nate weren't close."

Busted.

Faye thought quickly.

"She still knew him. Nate's family had been over to our house before. It was still traumatic for her."

Paula nodded. "You're right. I'm sorry. I can't imagine what she's going through."

"It's gotten to the point where she needed to stop going to school in person, and is now enrolled in virtual school."

Paula looked to the house. "She's home now?"

"Sleeping," Faye said quickly. "Her doctors don't want any added stress in her fragile state. I'm afraid that talking with you about Nate could be too much for her. At least for right now."

"I'm so sorry to hear about that. Must be so hard for you to watch, as her mom." Paula put a hand on her arm.

"It really is. I'm just glad I can stay home and be with her."

"Of course."

A red sedan pulled up to the curb.

Faye glanced at the time. "Speaking of my job, that's my next client. I'll be sure to give you a call if my kids tell me anything that could point you to Nate."

"I appreciate that."

She dumped the pulled weeds into the yard waste container and hurried inside.

Paula might be a problem.

Faye would have to figure out what to do about her if she came around again. She needed to keep that woman away from her kids.

Chapter Fourteen

BRAD HANDED his menu to the waiter and turned to Scott, his curiosity burning. What did he know about Ralf and Kurt that Brad had missed?

After Scott ordered his food, Brad turned to him. "What's your theory?"

"Like I said before, Ralf has a back-up plan. No doubt about that. If Kurt is out of the running for taking over his empire, there's a number two man. Or woman."

"He doesn't have any other children?"

"None that we know of."

Brad tilted his head. "You think he could have others?"

"Someone like him? Without a doubt."

That was something Brad hadn't considered, but it did make sense. Ralf wouldn't leave his life's work up to chance. He was like an old-time mob boss.

What didn't make sense was the connection to the car wash. Ralf had admitted to Brad that there *was* a link between the two, but had said it wasn't what Brad thought.

Scott set down his glass. "What are you thinking?"

"Trying to make sense of it all. Do you know what the Slippery Fish has to do with all this?"

"They're the ones behind your neighbor's murder?"

Brad nodded. "Rose was working with Wes Campbell."

"Campbell was one of the car wash's operatives?"

"Yes, and my neighbor. The whole point of that killing was to make me look guilty."

"And there were hits put out on you?" Scott scratched his chin.

"While I was on assignments. But I managed to take out the hitmen and my targets."

"Nice. No wonder Ralf has you running things."

"Until he decides to put out another hit on me. What do you think?"

"Ralf runs both. Think about it. If one company goes down, then he has the other. It's the perfect insurance plan."

Brad blinked a few times. He'd contemplated that possibility, but hearing Scott say it out loud made seem it more obvious.

Scott continued. "Why else would there be *two* such businesses here in Pine Harbor? He's keeping it all close, where he can keep an eye on everything. Think about it. This is a clean little place with no other real crime to speak of."

"That's what makes it the ideal place. Nobody's going to question the business fronts."

"But there are plenty of other towns like this. If there really was another company, why come here? And why wouldn't Ralf run the other one out of town, if he was here first? You really think he'd just put up with that kind of competition? It's too risky."

Brad raked his fingers through his hair, the reality of everything settling in.

Brad becoming an assassin was no coincidence. The Bergmanns wanted him close, where they could control him. That's why Ralf had been so willing to put him in charge.

He was keeping his friends close and his enemies closer.

Brad started to say something about his dad's killing, but stopped. How did he know that he could trust Scott? He could easily be on Ralf's side, trying to make Brad feel comfortable. Trying to get him to open up.

This could all be a trap.

Ralf might not care if Brad knew he was running the other assassination business. Or maybe he wasn't, and Scott had made up the entire story to satisfy Brad's curiosity on the matter.

He couldn't trust anyone. Least of all Scott. He'd been with the company even longer than Brad. Was older and more experienced.

And he wasn't even remotely bothered by the fact that Brad was now sitting behind Kurt's desk, when in reality it should've been Scott. He was the more senior member of BlueBlade.

"What are you thinking?" asked Scott.

"I'm not sure yet. It's all only starting to sink in."

Scott nodded. "I understand. I've had my entire sabbatical to think about it. Now I'm convinced. It's the only thing that makes any sense."

"It does seem that way."

The waiter brought over their food, providing a much-needed break in the conversation.

As Brad ate his soup — chicken swimming a green curry broth — he watched Scott from the corner of his eye.

Scott wasn't giving off any signals of deceit or nervousness. Seemed overly relaxed while lost in thought.

It was possible the other man was being authentic. However, it was also just as likely that he was Ralf's man.

Brad would play along. Pretend he believed everything Scott said.

But he was going to work on his own.

He couldn't trust anyone.

Chapter Fifteen

HADLEY STARED out her window as the high schoolers piled out of the bus, laughing and poking each other. Hard to believe that used to be her. Felt like a million years ago when she was so carefree.

Back when Duke was still alive.

She felt like crying as she glanced over at his old house, now the home of a young family. The parents had asked her about babysitting, and while she normally would've said yes, she didn't think she could bring herself to go inside.

Ever.

The last time she'd gone over was shortly after his death. It had been cathartic to be around his things, to lie in his bed, to smell him.

Now it was all gone. Duke's relatives had taken his things from the house. New people lived in the rooms he'd spent so much time in.

His bedroom, where he'd died at the hands of Rose and Wes.

Wes had killed the love of Hadley's life, and she'd killed his son.

It was kind of poetic.

Even though she hadn't meant to kill Nate. That was the last thing she'd ever wanted to do. The knife had been meant as a defense against Wes.

Hopefully, if nothing else, now he regretted threatening her. It was his fault his son had died.

Relief washed over her like a cool waterfall on a hot summer day.

She'd thought about it over and over, but there had always been a part of her that didn't really believe Wes was responsible. But this was the first time Hadley believed it.

If Wes hadn't treated Hadley the way he had, Nate *would* still be alive. She'd have had nothing in her possession that could have killed him.

She really was innocent. It hadn't been anything other than an accident. How could it be otherwise? She didn't want Nate dead, no matter what he'd done.

Hadley collapsed onto the floor, gasping for air as the guilt lifted and floated away.

It wasn't enough to fix everything, but it was enough to move forward.

She pulled herself up and gathered some clothes. It was time for a shower. She couldn't remember the last time she'd had one. Ratched had allowed her a few, but she'd been stingy with even something so basic as hygiene.

Not that it mattered now. Hadley was home, and she was never going back there.

Today was the first day of the rest of her life. She smiled, even though it was so cliché. It really was a new beginning.

A sucky one, but she'd take it.

Life was moving on, whether she liked it or not. She

might as well try to get with the program. If she wanted to graduate with her class — that was a big if at this point — she needed to catch up on virtual school. Or she could do online summer school. Either way.

Her first step was to get a shower. Maybe put on a little makeup. Even just some mascara and colored lip gloss would feel great.

By the time she stepped out of the shower, she felt like a new person. It wouldn't last forever, that much she knew, but she wanted to go with it while she could. At her vanity, she applied not only mascara and gloss, but also some eyeliner and blush.

She pictured Duke standing behind her, smiling. Kissing her neck and telling her she was beautiful.

Hadley closed her eyes and held onto the image until it slowly evaporated.

Once it did, she pulled her damp hair back into a ponytail and headed downstairs.

It was so nice to be able to choose her own food. She could rummage through the fridge and cabinets, and take whatever she wanted. Plus, the food here was *so* much better than the stuff slopped on her plate back at the hospital.

Just as she sat down with a plate of reheated brisket and potatoes, the front door squeaked open.

Zeke laughed as he slammed it shut.

Her heart warmed. She hadn't seen him the night before — everyone else was in bed when she and her parents finally made it home.

Hadley could hardly believe how much she'd missed him, not that she'd realized it until that moment.

She leaped up and hurried into the hall.

He turned, his eyes widening. "You're back."

Hadley raced over and threw her arms around him. "You can't get rid of me that easily."

Zeke returned the embrace. "Good."

The doorknob jiggled, and they both jumped back.

Wynn stepped inside, looked at Hadley. "You are alive. I was starting to think Zeke had offed you." He laughed.

Neither Hadley nor Zeke did.

Hadley took a few steps down the hall. "I'm going to eat."

"We're going to play a round for my gaming channel," Zeke said.

"You got that set up?"

He beamed. "Yeah. It's going amazing — you should see all the followers I have."

Wynn nudged him. "Even picked up some trolls."

"What trolls?" Hadley asked.

Zeke's ears reddened. "Nothing."

"It isn't nothing." Wynn poked him. "You've got people—"

"Shut up!" Zeke turned to Hadley. "Really, it's nothing." Then he grabbed Wynn's arm and dragged him up the stairs.

Hadley shook her head as she made her way into the kitchen. Those two were always up to something.

It sounded like a body slammed into the floor upstairs.

Always up to something.

She couldn't help smiling. The annoyances here were a welcome change from all the crazy drama back at the hospital.

Ding-dong!

More of Zeke's friends? It was usually just Wynn coming over to hang out, but that might've changed too.

She took a few more bites of her food.

Zeke didn't race down the stairs to answer the door, and the bell didn't ring again.

Probably a package. Or maybe one of Mom's clients. It was hard to remember she had her salon running now.

Ding-dong!

Hadley looked at her half-empty plate of food and sighed.

Looked like it was up to her to answer the door.

She took another bite, went back to the entry, and peeked outside.

Some guy was standing on the porch, though she couldn't tell who.

Hadley opened the door, and as she did, he turned toward her.

Duke.

It couldn't be.

Her heart skipped a beat. Then another. She clung to the door frame.

There was no way he was Duke.

He stepped closer. "Hi, Hadley."

It wasn't Duke — this guy had the same color hair, and the same build, and even his smile reminded her of Duke, but he didn't have her true love's dimples.

She wasn't losing her mind.

The guy continued. "I don't know if you remember me. I helped you into the store at the accident."

From the accident. It all made sense now. She'd even thought he reminded her of Duke then.

"Yes, of course I remember you."

"I've been thinking about you since that night."

"You have?"

He nodded, holding her gaze, his eyes as kind as they were that horrible night. "It's been hard not to worry, between the blood and how upset you were. But I'm glad you're home now. That's good news, right? To be out of the hospital."

"Yeah. Just got back last night." Her face warmed slightly. Did he know what kind of a hospital she'd spent most of the time in?

He flashed her an easy smile, almost as infectious as Duke's. "Such a relief. You look like you're doing better."

"Being home helps."

"I'm sure it does." He glanced at his watch. "My name's Rick, by the way. I have to get going, but if you ever want to talk or hang out, give me a call."

He wanted to hang out with her?

"Um, yeah. That sounds great, but I don't have your number."

He dug into his jeans pocket and pulled out a business card. "Now you do. And don't worry about the time — call as early or late as you need. I've been through some accidents myself, and I know how traumatic they can be."

She glanced down at the card. It said he worked in protection services.

He was a bodyguard.

"Okay. And thanks for your help that night, if I didn't say it that night."

"Just glad I was there to help." He smiled again before leaving.

Hadley went back inside.

What just happened? And why did he care so much?

She didn't have the answers, but in a way it felt like Duke was reaching out to her from wherever he was. And she liked it.

Chapter Sixteen

BRAD'S PHONE buzzed with a text. He wanted to throw both his cell phone and the office phone across the room.

They wouldn't stop going off. Between Ralf and the agent, he was going to lose his mind.

Ralf was demanding more progress on the targets he'd passed along to Brad to hand out to the assassins. And yet, at the same time, Bancroft had ordered Brad to make sure none of those people were killed.

Having two opposing bosses was going to land him in the hospital with a prescription for blood pressure medicine.

His phone buzzed again. Before chucking it, he glanced at the screen.

Faye. She wanted him to call her.

He breathed a sigh of relief. He'd much rather speak with her than either of his bosses.

Brad called, and she answered on the first ring. "Are you almost home?"

"I'm getting ready to leave."

"You're still at the office?" she exclaimed.

"Unfortunately." He pushed the chair back and gathered his things. "But I'm about to leave."

"Can you pick up some soda from the store? We don't have much in the way of drinks to offer Richard."

Pressure built behind Brad's eyes. With everything going on at work he'd forgotten about his mom's new friend coming over for dinner. He'd looked into the guy that morning, but found nothing. Not even a speeding ticket. On paper, he appeared to be a perfect citizen.

But paper meant nothing. People had other ways of hiding things.

"Are you there?" Faye asked.

"Yeah, I'll pick up some drinks. I'd better get going."

"Thanks, Brad. And your mom says thanks, too. She's excited about us having him over for dinner."

"It's no problem. See you soon." He ended the call and headed to his car.

Though he was too tired to deal with having anyone over, at least it gave him a chance to grill Richard. Try to poke holes in his perfect story. Find out what his angle really was. Why was he really going after Brad's mom?

He stopped off at the nearest grocery store and picked up enough drinks to feed an army. Got not only pop, but sparkling cider and wine, too. May as well have options. And if he could get Richard sipping wine, it'd be easier to get honest answers out of him.

By the time he got home, Faye and his mom were already setting the table.

Mom took one look at the bags of drinks and smiled at him. "Thanks for stopping to get those. I want to make this dinner nice."

Brad glanced at the food. "It looks like quite the feast."

"You don't think it's overboard? Maybe I should put away the—"

"No, Mom. It's fine."

It was strange seeing her worry so much over a meal. Like she was having pre-date jitters.

The thought made him shudder. That was his mom. The independent woman who'd been living on her own for the last three decades, who now couldn't stay alone.

Although since Brad had been in charge of her medications, taking the time to double-check each one online, her mental capacity had improved.

She was probably right about being able to handle the stairs to move back into the guest room. Or even her own house.

What if she was thinking about moving Richard in with her? Or her into his place?

He shook his head. They were only having the man over for dinner.

Brad set out the drinks on the counter.

Ding-dong!

He drew a deep breath.

Faye and his mom hurried toward the front door. Conversation sounded, then laughter.

Footsteps thundered down the stairs as the kids made their way down.

More talking and joking.

Richard sure knew how to woo people.

He wouldn't win Brad over so easily.

As everyone piled into the kitchen, Richard gave Brad a friendly smile and shook his hand. "You have a beautiful house."

"Thank you." Brad tried to smile. "I'm glad you could make it on such short notice."

"Considering I eat dinner alone every night, it wasn't hard to change my plans. Plus, there's no chance I'd turn down a home-cooked meal." He sniffed the air. "It smells delicious."

"That it does. How long have you been a widower?"

"It's been just over a year, but it feels much longer."

"Must be lonely."

"The pets help to distract me. My daughters also bring over the grandkids a few times a month, sometimes more. They're definitely the highlight of any day."

"I bet."

Brad's mom came over and put her hand on Richard's arm. "Are you ready to eat?"

"I sure am."

She led him to the table, but he held out a chair for her and helped her sit, gently scooting her in.

He had the gentleman act perfected. No wonder he had Mom charmed.

Not to be outdone, Brad held out a chair for Faye. Then he opened a bottle of wine and two sparkling apple ciders.

Everyone spoke excitedly as they served themselves and began digging in.

Brad watched Richard, who helped his mom diligently while conversing with and entertaining everyone else. He couldn't help thinking this would've been what family dinners might've been like if his dad had lived to see Brad marry and have kids.

Sadness washed through him. Though his dad had been gone for so long, the grief never truly went away. Realizations like this one made it nearly as hard as when it first happened.

All the more reason to kill Ralf.

Brad might be done with assassinations now that he was working with Bancroft, but he still had one more mission. He would get the information that the agent needed to take down Ralf's murderous empire.

Then he would make Ralf pay for what he'd done. He wasn't going to escape that easily. Not like Kurt, who had gotten off with prison.

Ralf would be Brad's final kill, and he would know exactly who was taking his life and why.

Brad's thirty-year journey would finally be over.

Then he could figure out what to do with the rest of his life. It would be hard to focus on something else after so long. But it would also be a relief. A new start.

The rest of the evening with Richard went off without a hitch. The man didn't give Brad any indication that he had ulterior motives, and he treated everyone like royalty.

Richard was either the real deal, or he was an extremely talented actor. Given what Brad had found on him, it was likely the former.

Perhaps after three decades, his mom was finally opening herself up to love. Brad would support her as long as Richard remained as good as he appeared so far. Not everyone was a devious killer.

Brad, Faye, and his mom saw their guest to the door after a few rounds of Scrabble.

Richard smiled at Brad. "Thank you for having me over. I've enjoyed getting to know your family."

Brad shook his hand. "It was a pleasure having you. I hope you can come again."

"I'd like that very much." He turned to Brad's mom, with a sparkle in his eyes. "As usual, I enjoyed my time with you. I hope to see you tomorrow at the center."

"You definitely will." She beamed.

Richard's hand lingered on hers for a moment before he stepped outside and wished everyone a good night.

"I appreciate you having him over." His mom gave them each a hug before retreating to her temporary room.

Faye nudged Brad. "Do you still think he has ulterior motives?"

"It's looking less and less likely, but I haven't ruled anything out yet."

She snorted. "Will anyone ever be good enough for your mom or daughters?"

"Probably not."

Faye looped her arm around his and turned to her salon. "Do you think it's possible to connect the security system in there?"

"If someone breaks in there, it'll alert the police just like any other door or window in the house."

"But I mean, a way to access it inside. You know, like a way to set it off if something goes sideways with one of my clients."

"Did something happen?"

"I'm just thinking about the future. It's me alone with whatever clients book appointments. I know it's built so they can't get into the house from there, but what if I feel threatened?"

Brad frowned. "Are you sure nothing happened? Remember, no more secrets."

She sighed. "No, nothing *happened*. I was cutting a guy's hair today, and it got me thinking."

He studied her, trying to figure out if she was hiding anything. But he was probably reading too much into it, since he was already on edge about everything else. "I'll look into it tomorrow."

"Thank you." She threw her arms around him.

"You'd tell me if something happened, wouldn't you?"

"Yes. I'm only thinking ahead."

He hoped she was telling the truth.

Chapter Seventeen

Zeke checked his new comments as he waited for his newest video to upload. His subscriber count was still climbing by the day.

Not only that, but the comments were getting to the point that it was almost too much to keep up with. He had time to like each one, but definitely didn't have the time to respond to them all. Only the best ones.

He also had to delete a few every day. Most were jealous kids with nothing better to do than put down someone better than them. There were a few trolls.

JimBob kept coming back, no matter how many times Zeke deleted his comments and blocked him. The guy just made a new account with different numbers tacked onto his name. He wanted Zeke to know it was him each time.

And there it was. Near the end of the comments. The new JimBob message. It was almost the same as the one he'd read on the bus, but even more obnoxious this time.

JimBob2000: I no who the real assassin is. It isn't ur character. Who's ur daddy? Liking his new promotion? Bet he is.

Zeke deleted and banned him again. For all the good that would do. He would just show up again the next day.

The cursor bounced around the screen as his shaking hand unintentionally moved the mouse.

How did the troll know about his dad being the boss? Was it a lucky guess? Or did he actually know that his dad now ran BlueBlade? Or was he referring to something else in the assassin business that Zeke didn't know anything about?

Could the troll be an assassin?

That thought sent an icy chill through him. If that were true, that meant a trained killer was focused on Zeke.

And he couldn't tell his dad about it. Not if he wanted to keep his gaming channel. Dad would freak if he knew about the troll.

He could also help. No doubt he'd know what to do. Might even know who was behind it.

But it was too big of a risk. His dad could make him shut down the channel. And there was no way he was doing that. It had been his dream for as long as he could remember. He'd spent too much time saving for the equipment. Put so much effort into building his following. More and more people were watching him play live.

Money was already starting to roll in. Mom had set up a checking account for him to collect earnings, and it was already double what he'd started with. Once he figured out the whole ad thing, it would double again soon.

He was not putting all of his work at risk by mentioning any of this to Dad. Not for a lone troll.

Maybe it was someone from the neighborhood who knew just enough to make chilling accusations. Or one of Dad's coworkers.

There was also another possibility. One Zeke didn't want to think about.

But it was also one he couldn't ignore.

It could be Wynn. His best friend knew about his dad's real job. He even knew about the promotion. And he had every reason to be jealous, since his parents wouldn't let him start a gaming channel. Wynn might even resent the threats Dad had made after he found out that Wynn knew about him being an assassin.

The thought of the troll being his best friend sucked. He didn't even want to consider the possibility, real as it so obviously was.

If Zeke brought it up and Wynn had nothing to do with it, that could end their friendship. On the other hand, if his friend *was* the troll, that would also put an end to everything.

They'd been friends ever since they were little. Been through all kinds of things together. Zeke had been there for him when his parents split and then again through each new love interest his parents brought home. Wynn had stood by Zeke's side all throughout the mess of people accusing his dad of murdering Duke and Allison. They'd both been there for each other through the years of bullying.

That's why it didn't make sense that his friend would use sensitive information against him. Why put their life-long friendship on the line?

Unless he was really that jealous, and he didn't care about losing their friendship. In a school where they were both the biggest outcasts, they always stuck together.

Or they *had*. Was it possible that had changed? Or that Wynn saw it that way? Could he be pushing Zeke away out of fear that Zeke would forget him once his popularity soared?

But that was crazy. It wasn't like the gaming channel

was scoring him any points at school. The whole incident with Lance on the bus was proof enough of that.

People were talking about that all over social media. Lance had threatened to get Zeke back when he least expected it.

His gaming channel had done nothing for his social life. At least not yet.

Did Wynn really think that would change anything between them?

If he was behind the JimBob persona, then it already had.

Either way, Zeke had to get to the bottom of the troll issue. Whether it was his best friend or a trained assassin, it was up to him to find out what was going on, without letting anyone else know what he was doing.

There was zero room for mistakes.

Chapter Eighteen

FAYE SIPPED her espresso as she studied the hair dryers on the grocery store shelf. Hers had died that morning while doing her hair, and she needed a replacement before her first client. She needed something professional-grade, but that would have to wait. Nothing was open this early, and she needed *something*. So, a crappy one would have to be good enough for the time being.

She finally settled on one that was a ripoff of a pricey model. Hopefully, none of her clients would notice before she was able to get a true replacement. And if they did, she would explain what happened. Surely, they'd understand. And she'd make sure to purchase a back-up to prevent this from happening again.

After purchasing the hair dryer, she hurried to the exit. Just as she stepped outside, someone blocked her path.

Paula.

Was the woman following her?

"Excuse me." Faye stepped to the side.

Paula moved in front of her. "Do you have a minute?"

"No. I need to get to work. My first client will be there

any minute." She stepped to the other side.

Blocked again.

That was when she noticed Paula's eyes were bloodshot and her hair wild. "Have you had a chance to speak with your kids about Nate yet?"

Faye drew a deep breath, trying to keep her cool. "I did, and like I said before, I'll call you if I learn anything that could help."

Paula stared at her. "I need answers."

"I'm sure you do. If one of my kids were missing, I'd be desperate, too."

"Your daughter has to know something. She was the last person to talk to him!"

"That doesn't mean anything. And to clarify, she's the last person *seen* speaking with him. Nate could've run into anybody after that."

"They were arguing!" Paula's eyes shone with tears.

"Kids argue. It happens all the time. I wish it led to something useful in finding Nate, but it didn't. They had a spat, and unfortunately, that was the last time anyone saw him — including Hadley. All the people who watched them interact also saw her leave on her own."

"Look, I've been as nice as I can be about this but I'm at the end of my rope. I need answers, and your daughter has them. You need to let me talk to her. I won't do anything other than ask questions."

"If you really want to know what happened, you should visit the guy who was arrested for the crime. He'd be the one who knows whether Nate is alive or not."

Tears spilled onto Paula's face. "He hasn't admitted to anything this far. Not to the authorities, not to anyone."

"Maybe seeing your grief would move him to talk."

She narrowed her eyes. "It hasn't worked for you."

Faye clenched her fists. "I'm not hiding anything."

"Sure you're not."

"Are you accusing me of something? Because if you are, come out and say it."

"I've been saying it all along. Your daughter knows something."

Anger boiled in Faye's chest. "What does she know? If you're so sure, why don't you tell me?"

"If I knew, I wouldn't be looking for answers!"

Faye stepped closer, gritting her teeth. "You need to look elsewhere. Have you tried speaking with Wes? That man had a temper, and he was known for threatening people. He even killed his wife!"

"He was in *jail* when Nate disappeared."

"Doesn't mean he didn't have anything to do with it. Inmates still make contact with the outside world, you know. And what about the aunt who was so eager to move the kids away from their home? Have you accused her of anything?"

"You mean the woman who was suddenly given custody of three kids, and wanted to get back to her own home? She sounds like a saint to me."

"All I know is that you need to leave my family alone. Don't go near my kids. If you do, there will be trouble. That much I can assure you."

"Are you threatening me?"

"I'm telling you to leave my family alone. Someone is in jail for his part in Nate's disappearance — and it isn't us. It's never been us! The police department has accused my husband of numerous murders. And he was proven innocent of them all. In fact, Wes was responsible for most of them. Give *him* a harder look if you're serious about finding answers. You're not going to find them by harassing my family."

Paula's eyes shone with tears again. "I don't know

where else to turn. My dream was always to find Nate after he turned eighteen and graduated, but now it looks like I'll never have that opportunity. All I want is answers."

"I feel for you, I do. But you need to stop pestering my family. I have three kids to think about, myself, and one of them isn't holding up so well. I'll let you know if I hear anything useful, but you need to leave us alone. Do you promise to do that much?"

Paula took a step back, wiping her eyes. "You really think Wes had something to do with it?"

"Wouldn't surprise me. Do you promise to leave us alone?"

She sighed, frowned. "It's hard. Everyone I talk to brings up your family."

"And that automatically makes us guilty?"

"It means I have to ask."

"Do you know how much stress that adds to the trauma we're already dealing with?" Faye looked at the time. "I have to get going, or I'm going to risk losing a client. I would *like* to help, but you have to let us come to you. Not the other way around. Can you do that?"

"Looks like I'm going to have to." Paula walked away, her head hung low.

Faye's heart hammered.

She needed to figure out what to do if Nate's mom didn't keep her word. She doubted the police would do anything, and it wasn't like she could stop the woman from showing up in the same public places that Faye frequented. Brad might want to have the woman taken care of — and even if he didn't overreact to her snooping, he'd be openly hostile, which would only make the woman more certain they were hiding something.

If Paula persisted, Faye would have to deal with the woman on her own.

Chapter Nineteen

BRAD WOKE with knots in his stomach. It was finally Saturday. The day he was going to kill his father's murderer.

The week had dragged on, feeling like two or three. Made worse by his mom's love interest, but he had to admit that having Richard over for dinner had set his mind at ease. He was still looking into his past, but the man appeared to be a lonely widower looking for companionship.

"Can you turn your alarm off?" asked Faye.

Brad reached for his phone and pushed the button on the side to make it stop.

Faye rolled over, and for a moment he was jealous, wishing he could sleep in. But he had more important matters to attend to. Like killing Ralf.

He was ready for anything. If his boss checked for weapons and took Brad's gun and knife, he wouldn't find the thin metal wire Brad had tucked into his belt. No way anyone would find that, and it could be just as effective to garrote Ralf as to shoot him.

It was just a matter of getting himself alone with the old man. He didn't need a lot of time, but he couldn't be anywhere near the other assassins.

That would be the tricky part. But he wasn't going to let the opportunity slip between his fingers.

Today would be everything.

Afterward, he would need to figure out the rest of his life. A new career — he wanted nothing to do with either knives or killings. Unfortunately, Brad had been at this so long, he didn't know anything else.

But thinking about it now was only procrastinating. The only thing he needed to focus on was taking out Ralf. If he didn't do that, he wouldn't have to worry about finding a new career.

He kept his thoughts focused as he got ready for the day. As he stepped into the hall, he heard cartoons downstairs and smelled pancakes and bacon.

His stomach rumbled. May as well eat something before leaving, in case he had the opportunity to take care of Ralf before he served breakfast.

Noise came from Zeke's room, which concerned him. His son usually slept past eleven on weekends.

Brad rapped on the door quickly before opening it.

His son sat at his desk playing his video game. Wynn sat next to him, cheering him on.

It was like he'd gained another son, the kid was over so often. But since Wynn knew about Brad being an assassin, it *was* best to keep him where he could see him.

"Why are you two up so early?"

Wynn glanced back. "Huge event this weekend. Can't let the people on the East Coast get the advantage."

Zeke held up a hand, indicating for them to stop talking.

Wynn rolled his eyes. "You can edit us out of your video."

"Do you record everything you play?" Brad asked.

Zeke waved his hand around.

Wynn nodded. "It all goes up. He's got followers who'll watch everything."

Brad stepped inside. "You don't ever talk about *family business* on there, do you?"

Zeke yanked off his headphones and glared at him. "Of course not. Would you let me play? This tournament is important. I'm going to get a ton of views, which means loads of money from ads. I finally got those figured out."

Brad started to step out, but hesitated. "How many people watch you?"

His son sighed dramatically. "Thousands. Can I get back to this now?"

"And anyone can watch?"

Zeke rolled his eyes. "Seriously? Yes. They're public videos, that's how I make money."

"And you have fans?"

"*Yes.*"

"People who could get obsessed and come to the house?"

"I'm not that popular."

"But you could get stalkers."

"Hypothetically. But nobody cares that much." Zeke threw his friend a pleading look.

Wynn sat up straight. "He has haters, people who definitely wouldn't ever come to the house."

Zeke shoved him.

"Haters?" Brad asked.

"Just some stupid trolls," Zeke said. "Making stupid comments. It's nothing. Everyone gets them."

Wynn raised a brow. "What about the one who keeps commenting about assassins?"

"What?" Brad exclaimed.

"It's *nothing*!" Zeke's face reddened. "Just people being stupid."

"Someone knows about the assassinations?"

"No," Zeke snapped. "They're referring to the assassins in the game. You read too much into things. Don't you have to get to your boss's house for your big breakfast?"

Brad checked the time, annoyance running through him. "Yes. We're going to talk about your trolls when I get back."

Zeke glared at Wynn. "Thanks *so* much."

"What did I do?" Wynn raised his hands.

Brad drew a deep breath and headed downstairs, his stomach still rumbling from the aromas of food.

Mom smiled at him from the stove. "You want something to eat? I started early, knowing you had plans this morning."

"Thanks." He gave her an appreciative smile. It was thoughtful of her, even though his plans already included breakfast. He asked her about Richard as he scarfed down scrambled eggs and bacon, and she spoke excitedly about their time at the center. Nothing sounded suspicious.

Then he hurried to the car, his stomach knotting again. At least he hadn't eaten much. Just enough to keep his stomach from growling. Enough to stay focused on what he needed to do.

But his mind kept returning to Zeke's trolls, especially the one who mentioned assassinations. Was it someone who knew about Brad's work? Or a random idiot behind a keyboard spewing nonsense?

Problem was, it could go either way. Someone in his

line of work could easily figure out that Zeke was Brad's son and mess with him.

Brad shook his head to clear it.

Time to focus.

Why did he have to be so distracted on such an important day? He'd been dreaming of avenging his father for thirty years. And yet all these other thoughts were forcing their way in, demanding attention. At least Hadley was home. That was one less thing to worry about.

Brad pulled up to the curb in front of the Bergmanns' enormous house. The driveway was already packed with cars.

It was going to be quite the event.

What was Ralf planning? Was he going to make an announcement? Restructure the business now that his son was in prison?

He checked his gun, his knife, and the metal wire. All in place. Each one ready in case it was the ideal weapon when the moment finally came. He also had the electronic wire, to capture anything damning coming out of Ralf's mouth. That, too, was in place.

Brad sent a quick text to the agent, letting her know he was at the location.

She texted him back, letting him know that she was ready to listen and offer any assistance.

Another car pulled up as Brad got out of the car.

Scott.

Brad waved and headed up the driveway. The front door opened before he reached the porch.

Ralf stood there, more tanned than ever, smiling and waving him in. "Good morning. Hope you're hungry. We have a full spread."

He was anything but hungry, but he grinned. "Can't wait. Thanks for the invitation."

Ralf looked behind Brad and waved. "Scott! Come on in."

No matter how many times Brad had been in the large home, its vastness always took him by surprise. If it wasn't technically a mansion, then it was close, barely missing the required square footage.

He looked around, trying to look past the expensive everything, and into where he might find what the agent needed. A safe could be hiding behind any framed picture or art piece.

Brad wasn't nearly as worried about cameras here. If he was able to kill Ralf, he would also be able to find and destroy the recording equipment.

Conversation sounded from the dining room. Nearly a dozen men sat around the large table. Brad knew all but a few of them. Most wore suits, or at least ties. Brad was underdressed for the occasion — whatever it was. Just breakfast? Something else entirely?

He'd find out soon enough. But at least he'd worn a button-up shirt and slacks. He wasn't entirely out of his element.

Brad greeted everyone and took one of the empty seats. Most seemed in good spirits, with plenty of smiles to go around. The food was plentiful, which wasn't surprising. The Bergmanns always went overboard, and it appeared the father outdid the son.

More voices sounded toward the front door. Two more men entered. Brad didn't recognize them.

He turned to Scott. "How many of these guys do you know?"

"About half."

Less than Brad. That didn't make him feel better. Those he didn't recognize were undoubtedly from the Slippery Fish, but why was Ralf suddenly bringing the two operations together, after years of running them in parallel?

Did he fear a coup? Was he hoping to play one group against the other? Or were the Slippery Fish assassins there to protect him from Brad, and anyone else Brad might have persuaded to follow his lead?

Anything was a possibility.

Before he could kill Ralf, he needed to get his boss to say something that the agent would consider valuable. Then, ideally, he would kill the old man quietly, hide the body, and go through the house once the other guests left.

Chances were, the ideal plan wouldn't be an option.

Ralf entered the room with another man and sat at the head of the table while everyone else watched in silence. "I'm so glad you're all here. It's time for you to learn the truth."

Chapter Twenty

BRAD LEANED as close to Ralf as he could, reaching for a soufflé so he wouldn't look suspicious.

So far, Ralf had only talked about the history of the business. He didn't mention BlueBlade, or any other company, as he discussed his passion for keeping the world a safe place, all in the name of avenging his daughter's murder.

It was ironic. He got into the business for the same reason as Brad — to repay the death of a loved one. And that was also what would get him killed that very day, if Brad had anything to say about it.

Brad didn't respond. Waited for the old man to stop droning on. And on. He talked about the business as if it were one company, although he didn't refer to it as Blue-Blade or the Slippery Fish. Was this his way of announcing a merger?

Not that it mattered.

Vengeance. That was what mattered. That, and getting the information the agent needed. But he could do that before or after killing his father's murderer.

Ralf pointed to one of the men he was praising, and everyone else applauded. Brad reluctantly joined in, hoping the speech was over.

But if anything, it sounded like things were just getting started.

The man was as long-winded as he was old. He told multiple stories about each man at the table, stopping only to allow applause.

At this rate, all of Brad's kids would be out of the house by the time this was done. And his stomach would burst from all the food. He was trying to distract himself by eating more, and more, and more.

Ralf finally turned his attention to Brad.

He could hardly pay attention to the story shared, about a challenging target that Brad had barely managed to kill in his early days. Brad couldn't figure out what Ralf's angle was, though he did his best to smile and react to his boss's tones and inflections. Then more applause.

Was this something Ralf did regularly, but Brad had never been invited? Or was there more to it? Nobody else seemed concerned or suspicious.

Unless they were in on it, too. Whatever *it* was.

After talking about Brad, Ralf was finally finished. He sat and attended to his own plate of food, which was no doubt cold at this point. Conversation spread slowly around the table.

Brad pretended to eat even more food as he studied everyone.

The others were relaxed and verbally high-fiving one another for things Ralf had said.

Brad turned to Scott and praised him for the story Ralf shared about him.

Scott returned the favor.

That was exactly what this felt like.

Was that really what Brad was involved in? Not some elaborate illegal assassin ring, but a fringe religious group that was impossible to escape because everyone was a trained killer?

He made a mental note to ask the agent about that after taking out Ralf.

His heart raced at the thought.

A few minutes later, a man two seats down stood and thanked Ralf. Headed for the door.

Then another guy followed suit.

Was that it? An elaborate meal where the boss doled out compliments while everyone sweated in their best suits?

He could think of fifty better ways to spend a Saturday morning.

But the good news was, if the other assassins continued clearing the room, Brad's chance of success would soar. Fewer people to get in his way, less chance of something going wrong.

Unless some were planning on staying longer. That would put a wrinkle in his plot, but he would still find a way. If nothing else, he could pretend to see himself out, then sneak back in and wait for Ralf.

He was nothing if not patient. Sitting through the meal was proof enough of that.

One by one, others left the gathering. By the time the group had dwindled to half its size, nobody else showed any signs of leaving. Conversation continued, grew louder. Laughter roared in waves. One guy loosened his tie, then another.

Was Ralf expecting Brad to stay or leave? He wasn't indicating either way. Wasn't paying him any attention at all.

He also hadn't heard anything from Bancroft. Had she

gotten bored with listening in on the event, or was she waiting for Brad to make his move?

There was nothing he could do with so many others in the room. If it were just him and Ralf, that would be another story. But with a handful of top assassins still sitting around the table, his hands were tied.

Yet he needed to do something.

Brad rose.

Ralf turned to him. "Leaving so soon?"

He hadn't asked that of anyone else.

Brad shook his head. "Bathroom."

"You know where that is, right?"

"Yes." Brad hurried out of the room and went straight to the bathroom in case there were prying eyes or video cameras.

A text came in. The agent wanted to know if he was finally going to look for information.

Once in the bathroom, he sent her a message letting her know he was doing the best he could.

Then he darted down the hall and peeked into a few rooms. Most were locked. That would be where most of the good information was. Everything the agent wanted was likely to be next to impossible to get to.

"Lost?"

Brad whipped around, heart thundering, to face Ralf. "Yeah, actually. This place is huge."

"That's what I love about it. I used to get lost for the first full year I lived here."

Relief washed through Brad. If Ralf wasn't angry, he still had a chance.

"Let me show you something. You have a minute?"

"Of course."

Ralf led him down the hall and unlocked one of the doors near the end.

A vein in Brad's neck thrummed.

Ralf would likely see it when he turned around. Would know he was a bundle of nerves. He would suspect something.

Brad took deep, silent breaths as he followed Ralf into the dark room. One hand covered his neck, the other inched toward the gun. Then he changed his mind and moved toward the knife.

Too many people in the house. Close enough to hear a gun go off.

Ralf turned on the lights, exposing a home office. One not unlike Kurt's former office at BlueBlade. The furniture was even arranged similarly.

It was almost eerie how similar they were, but Kurt may have wanted to feel like he had one office, no matter where he was.

Brad forced a chuckle. "It's almost like stepping into the knife store."

"Isn't it? My son certainly has a specific style."

"That he does." Brad eyed Ralf, watching for any indication of his thoughts while the topic was on Kurt.

The agent was supposed to have silenced Kurt about Brad trying to kill him, but that didn't mean the father and son couldn't find some way to communicate.

Now Brad was alone with Ralf in a room with only one way out, and other assassins in the house.

Things could turn sideways quickly.

He could also finally kill his father's murderer, and be done with it.

Ralf made his way to the back of the room to a cabinet. In the other office, a bookshelf stood in its place. He pulled out a key and unlocked it.

Brad's vein pulsed again. He stepped nearer, his hand

again inching toward his knife. Checking the metal wire tucked into his belt.

He was set.

Ralf turned around a pulled out a book. Looked like a ledger.

"What's that?" Brad asked, his throat dry.

"My son is a meticulous note-taker. Has notes on everything and everyone from the last thirty years."

Was Ralf about to bring up his father?

Brad moved his hand from the knife to the gun. He would need something quicker, even if it was louder. Self-defense. The agent would get him off.

Only if she got the information she wanted. If he didn't find anything, she could leave him high and dry.

"Who did Kurt take notes on about thirty years ago?" Brad crept closer, staying behind Ralf, out of his line of vision.

"Plenty of people." He flipped through the pages, studying them intently.

"He must've been pretty young then. We're not too far apart, and I was in high school back then."

"Kurt was just out of high school." He continued flipping.

"That would've been about the time my dad was killed."

Ralf didn't so much as flinch. Didn't say anything, either.

Brad's phone buzzed with a text. He didn't have to look to know it was Bancroft, wanting him to get more information about the early days of the operation.

Ralf glanced at him. "Do you need to get that?"

"No. Just my wife checking in. You know how it is."

He scowled. "Sure do. That's why I got rid of my old lady long ago."

The words sent an icy chill through Brad. Had Ralf killed his wife? Did Kurt know?

Ralf turned back to the ledger.

Brad's phone buzzed again.

"She got you whipped?" Ralf asked.

"No." Brad flipped the little bar to silence his phone. He moved closer and looked at the open page. "You never did tell me how the Slippery Fish is connected to BlueBlade."

Ralf jolted.

"Remember, you said they're connected but not in the way I was thinking? Do some of those men out there belong with the car wash? Or is that the wrong connection?"

"You're quite observant." Ralf straightened his back. "I suppose that's how you ended up where you are."

Brad, blocked by the computer monitor, inched his fingers toward his gun. "Meaning in charge of BlueBlade?"

"Essentially."

"That doesn't answer my question. Are they both covers?"

"It doesn't concern you." Ralf's mouth twisted.

"What do I need to do to prove myself to you? Did you not mean all the complimentary things you just said about me to everyone else?"

Ralf rubbed his bald head, looking deep in thought.

Brad leaned a little closer, trying not to be obvious. He needed the agent to hear whatever Ralf said so that he could then kill the man. Anger pulsed through him as he thought about his dad's needless death, all the years stolen from him.

He shoved those thoughts aside. The only way he could

do what needed to be done was if he could stay focused on the task at hand. He couldn't falter now.

Ralf turned to him and leaned against the desk. "You're right."

Brad nearly choked on air. "About the connection?"

"Yes. They're both under my main umbrella company, but one would have an impossible time proving it. The paperwork and legalities are all in place to prevent anyone from discovering a link."

"Impressive." Brad widened his eyes, trying to hide the fact that he was lying through his teeth. "But people are always the downfall, right?"

Ralf tilted his head.

"I'd have never made the connection without Wes Campbell and Rose Flores. They killed my neighbors, which led to people pointing fingers at me. I had no other choice but to start doing my own digging."

"Yes, they were both problematic. Now they're never leaving prison. You can be sure of that."

"How do you know they won't say anything?"

"Because there are certain people they don't want killed. One word from them, and their loved ones will pay the price."

"Good insurance policy."

"The best."

"If I may be so bold, how many companies are there?"

Ralf studied him. "Enough that if one or two fold, my empire continues."

"Who takes over after you retire?" Brad's fingers reached the gun. His pulse quickened. Once he made the decision to act, he needed to be swift.

It was nothing he hadn't done hundreds of times before.

Except this was his boss.

His father's murderer.

Everything was on the line.

Ralf spoke, but with the blood rushing in his ears, Brad couldn't make out any of it. Hopefully it was something that would help the agent. Enough that she would forgive him for what had to be done.

He turned off the wire. Wrapped his fingers around the small gun. Slowly pulled it out of his pocket. Kept it behind the cover of the monitor. Nodded to Ralf as he paused between sentences. Moved his fingers into place. Acted natural. Didn't look down. Used his fingers to make sure everything was set.

It all was.

Brad raised it. Fingers in place.

All he had to do was pull the trigger. The bullet would go through the thin monitor and then through Ralf.

Then it'd be over.

Ralf was still talking. Fully distracted.

Brad put a little pressure on the trigger. It was ready to go.

He started to pull.

The door flew open.

Scott.

He stood right behind Ralf. The bullet would get him, too.

His face was pale and he had perspiration on his hairline. "It's Vince! We think he had a heart attack. Thomas already called 911."

Ralf and Scott raced out of the room.

Brad collapsed onto the chair.

So close.

Chapter Twenty-One

Hadley checked her texts after adding the final touches on her makeup. It felt good to be putting effort into how she looked again. Almost made her feel normal.

She'd been ignoring virtual school, the idea of catching up in the summer sounding more and more appealing every time she considered the possibility. It wasn't like she would be walking around the beach with Ellie and their other friends.

Nothing was ever going to be normal again. She might as well take the time to rest and recover — she needed it after spending what felt like months in the hospital, dealing with Nurse Ratched.

With any luck, that woman had been fired. Dr. Fallow and the others probably had no idea how horrible she was to the patients. If any good came from Hadley's stay there, at least it was that. Dr. Fallow had walked in on that psychopath torturing her.

Her phone sounded with a text.

Rick was ready to meet.

Hadley let him know she would leave in a few minutes.

Then she pulled up her favorite picture of Duke on her phone — she really needed to have some of these printed and framed.

She ran her finger over the image of his face and sighed. "It's not a date, and I'm not replacing you. I just need a friend. Hopefully you understand. If you were still here, I'd obviously be going to you. Actually, if you were still here, none of this would've ever happened. Everything would be perfect still. Now it's …"

Hadley sighed, unable to find the right word. Frustrated, she turned back to her mirror and double-checked her makeup before heading downstairs.

Mom was in the kitchen. Must be lunchtime already.

That had to be why Rick had wanted to meet at a restaurant. She'd thought it was for breakfast.

She had lost all sense of time since being in the mental hospital. Sleeping all kinds of weird hours.

"You're up." Mom smiled. "And wearing makeup."

"I'm going to meet a friend for lunch."

"What friend? Are you reconnecting with someone? Is it Ellie?"

She sighed. "Mom, no."

Mom lifted a brow. "Who, then?"

"Just a friend."

"Who is it? Have I met her?"

"No. I need to go. I'm going to be late."

"Where are you going?"

"To lunch. Why the fifth degree?"

"Third," Mom corrected. "And because I worry about you. I think I've earned that right ten times over."

"It's just lunch. I'd think you'd be happy I'm getting out."

"I am. Just curious about the timing. Who are you meeting?"

"Gotta go, or I'll be late. Bye, Mom." Hadley blew her a kiss and hurried outside before she could question her any further. If Mom found out that Hadley was meeting Rick, she'd never allow Hadley to leave.

Her parents would see him as another Duke. Same age, and he even looked like Duke.

It was so dumb how society would be okay with the relationships once Hadley had her next birthday, but now it was taboo. Not that she had a relationship with Rick. She just wanted to properly thank him for helping after the accident.

As she started her car, her phone sounded with a text.

Mom.

Ugh. She was suffocating. But at least nothing like those nurses.

Hadley sent her a quick text saying she wouldn't be gone long, and that she'd text her at the restaurant. Didn't mention who she was meeting.

Not like anything could happen. They would just be having a meal. Out in public, no less. She wasn't getting into his car or going to his place.

She couldn't do that to Duke anyway. Mom had nothing to worry about. She *should* be concerned about the fact that Hadley had no plans of falling in love ever again. She didn't want to get married or have a family anymore. Not without Duke.

The restaurant parking lot was packed. She had to drive around a few times to find a spot, and even then, she'd almost lost it to a rusty sedan.

Rick texted her that he was already at the table. She quickly found him next to a window overlooking a pond with some ducks splashing around.

He welcomed her with an easy smile. "You look like you're improving by leaps and bounds."

It was the makeup, but she wasn't about to tell him that. "Thanks."

They made small talk while looking over the menus. After they'd ordered, Rick leaned back in his chair. "What are your plans?"

"What do you mean?"

"Are you going back to school or work? Or will you take some time to recover?"

"Oh, that. I like the idea of taking the rest of the semester off and making it up this summer. Or even taking the summer off, too, and extending my graduation. Since I'm doing virtual school, it really doesn't matter. I'm not walking with my class."

"You couldn't if you wanted to?"

Hadley shrugged. "I don't really care. That type of thing used to matter to me, but with everything that's happened this year, my priorities have shifted."

"It's been a rough year?"

She laughed out loud. "To put it mildly."

Rick frowned. "I'm sorry to hear that."

"I just hope all the drama is over now."

"Like what? Unless you don't want to talk about it."

She drew in a deep breath. "I don't even want to *think* about it. My family's been put through the wringer this year. Mostly my dad and me. And my grandma, come to think of it. I'm sick of secrets, and I'm sick of people dying."

He frowned. "That sounds like a lot to deal with."

"What sucks is realizing how horrible people are. I used to be pretty optimistic, believing in the best of everyone. Now I know I was blind. So, so very blind."

"Are people really that bad?"

"Yes," she snapped. "Sorry. Until I'm shown otherwise, that's my reality."

"You had a lot of friends in school, didn't you?"

Hadley paused. How would he have known that? They only met at the accident, and then he showed up at her house. She hadn't mentioned anything about that and forgotten, had she?

Not that she could remember, but who knew what she'd said after the accident? She'd sobbed in his arms. Anything could've come out of her mouth. The whole thing was a blur.

"I only ask because you seem like the kind of person that others would be drawn to. I'm sure all the girls want to be you."

Her face warmed, and she looked outside, spotting a trail of baby ducks following their parents.

Luckily, the appetizers arrived. She didn't have to answer his question and admit to having once been popular and loved, only to be hated and despised now.

If only Ellie would hear her out. Everyone at school was following her lead now.

Rick grabbed a mozzarella stick and dipped it in the sauce.

Hadley followed suit, barely tasting the food, wondering what Ellie and her other old friends were doing now. Probably in the cafeteria eating their own lunches. They might be laughing at her, whether or not they knew about her stay in the mental hospital.

Everyone had hated her before she landed there. How much worse would it be if they found out?

"You okay?"

She pulled herself from her thoughts and focused on Rick. It was jarring how much he looked like Duke. His eyes had the same warmth. His nose even had the same shape.

It was almost like her boyfriend was back from the dead.

But that was ridiculous.

He tilted his head, and she remembered he'd asked something. If she was okay.

"Yeah, I'm fine. Just tired."

Rick picked up another mozzarella stick. "You seem lost in thought."

She sighed. "Guilty as charged."

"Anything good?"

Hadley laughed bitterly. "No. Just thinking about how life hasn't gone at all the way I planned."

"Isn't that the truth?"

She studied him. "You too?"

"I think it's part of the human condition — it happens to us humans, caused by other humans."

"It sucks."

"It can. But it can also be good."

"How?"

He took a sip of his water. "Things have a way of turning around eventually."

"I don't see how any of the stuff I'm dealing with can turn out good."

"Life has a funny way of righting wrongs."

Now he was even starting to *sound* like Duke. There had been plenty of times when she'd been in a funk and just wanted to gripe and complain, but Duke would start trying to cheer her up. It was annoying, but now she'd give anything to go back and let him be as chipper as he wanted.

"You don't think so?" Rick asked.

"Some things can't be undone. Like death."

Now she was getting morbid. Her only "friend" would probably run for the hills before the meal was served.

"That's true." Rick looked deep in thought for a moment. "But good can happen in life even while we still miss people who are no longer with us. They would want us to enjoy life."

"Have you lost someone?"

"Several people. Most recently, my brother. Never would have expected that. We were supposed to have families, and our kids were going to be as close to each other as we were."

Could it be that he reminded her of Duke because this was his brother?

"I'm so sorry. That's awful. How old was he?"

"Twenty-seven."

Just ten years older than her. Two years older than Duke had been. So, he wasn't Duke's brother. "That's so young."

"Tell me about it."

"How'd you get over it?" she asked.

"I'm not sure I ever will."

She gave him a double-take. "But you're carrying on with life, and I'd never guess that anything was wrong."

"The pain isn't as bad most days, but every so often it's just as strong as the night I heard the news."

Hadley was without words. That was what she was experiencing with Duke. Some days were better, while others were just as bad as at first.

Rick gave her a sad smile. "If you ever want to talk about it, feel free. I know what it's like to grieve."

Maybe things were starting to turn around, after all.

At least now she had a friend.

Chapter Twenty-Two

BRAD PULLED into his driveway and rubbed his temples. He'd been so close to killing Ralf.

So. Close.

But then Scott had to walk in. Get in the way.

He should've felt bad about Vincent having a heart attack. But he didn't know the guy. And the paramedics had said his vitals were good. He'd probably be fine.

Now he had to plan the whole thing over again. New place, new method.

His phone's screen lit up on the dash.

The agent was texting him again. Probably wanted to know why the listening device had cut out.

He wasn't going to admit to doing that on purpose. Not when she wanted Ralf Bergmann alive.

But he couldn't keep putting her off. He glanced at the slew of missed texts and calls before calling her. He needed to get this over with before he went inside to attempt a normal Saturday with his family.

It rang once.

"What the hell happened?" she answered.

"Hello to you, too."

"What happened?" the agent demanded.

"I'm not sure what you mean," he said. "Didn't you hear everything?"

"No! The feed cut."

"It did? Really?"

"What did you do? Did you kill him?"

So she knew that he still planned to do it.

"I assure you he's alive and well."

Unfortunately, that was the truth.

"Then what happened after he started telling you about the structure of his empire?"

Was that what Ralf had been rattling on about when Brad was preparing to kill him?

"Hello?" she demanded. "Are you there? Your phone isn't cutting out too, is it?"

"It's working fine. I'll have a look at the wire and let you know."

"Test it now."

"I just pulled up to my house. I'm exhausted, and I want to go inside."

"Now!"

He held back an annoyed sigh. "Give me a minute."

"Hurry."

Having two bosses was for the birds. As soon as he was done with all of this, he would look into what he could do to be his own boss. Then the only person ordering him around would be himself.

He waited a few moments before flipping the wire back on. Pulled it close to his mouth. "You say this thing isn't working?" he said loudly.

"It is *now*. What happened?"

"You tell me. It's your device."

She made an annoyed noise that barely sounded human.

"Did you get enough information? Now we know that the Bergmanns are behind not only the knife shop *and* the car wash, but other operations, too. Did you hear that much, at least?"

"Yes. You need to get him to admit to more. I don't care what it takes."

"I'll be sure to get right on that."

"Before Monday. I'll check in tonight."

"Tonight?" he exclaimed.

The call ended.

She couldn't be serious.

Hadley's car pulled up to the curb.

Brad craned his neck to see inside. Had she left the house, or had Faye taken the car somewhere?

It was his daughter. What was she doing out?

Stomach churning acid, he got out of the car and hurried to meet her on the sidewalk. "Where have you been?"

"Out with a friend. Why?" She closed her door and set the alarm.

"You're supposed to be home resting."

"Isn't it good for me to be out with people?"

"Who were you with?"

"Don't answer my question with a question."

He shoved his hands in his pockets, tried to remain calm. "It's my job to worry about you."

"Well, I'm fine. Better than fine, in fact." Her smile seemed forced.

Brad took a deep breath. "Who were you with?"

"You won't answer my question, I'm not answering yours." She stormed inside.

He started to call after her, but didn't have the energy.

Not after the morning he'd had.

The important thing was that she was safe at home now. Although it did concern him that she wouldn't say who she'd been with, it didn't need to be dealt with right now.

Inside, Faye was washing some lady's hair in the salon. His mom was in the backyard with Luna, throwing the ball for the dog. Zeke was in his room with Wynn.

Another kid that he'd deal with later. The first thing he wanted to do was get out of his slacks and stiff shirt. Then sleep off the stress and the heavy meal. Or maybe have a beer. That sounded good, too.

Once in comfortable clothes, he flopped onto the bed and closed his eyes. Enjoyed the silence.

Until his phone rang.

He resisted the urge to throw it against a wall. Opened one eye to see who was calling.

Ralf.

It was as though he were taunting him about the missed opportunity. No. The boss was likely calling to see if Brad was working on passing the targets to other assassins.

He accepted the call and closed his eyes again. "Brad here."

"Ralf. How many targets have you delegated so far?"

Bingo.

"I just got home."

"That's no excuse."

"It's on my to-do list. Don't forget I'm dealing with some pretty serious family stuff."

"Kurt may have been soft on you, but you aren't getting any pity from me, Morris. Deal with that on your own time. Now that you're running an entire operation, your first priority is doing my bidding."

Like hell it was. Brad bit his tongue.

"You there?" Ralf asked.

"I heard you."

"Doesn't sound like you did. Sounds like you're half asleep."

"I'm resting, yes."

"You can sleep when you're dead. Get to work. I'm going to check in soon. I expect progress."

"I'll have something to report to you."

"Don't forget I know where you live."

Brad sat up. "Excuse me?"

"You heard me."

His pulse raced. Ralf was seriously threatening him. His family.

"I might call in thirty minutes, or I might call in five hours. Either way, you need to have answers."

Brad drew in a slow breath. "Okay."

"We on the same page now?"

"Always have been."

"I'll be in touch."

The call ended.

Brad started to throw his phone, but stopped just short of releasing it. That would do no good. Especially with Ralf threatening his family.

He checked his recent calls and rang Bancroft.

"This will have to wait," she answered. "I'm busy looking into—"

"You need to give me something regarding Ralf's targets. I have to pass them off to other assassins, or he's coming to my house."

"Under no circumstance are you to harm anyone on the list you gave me."

"That doesn't help me."

"No? Then tell him you've given them to me. You

supposedly hired me as an assassin, right?"

Brad muttered under his breath. "Are you listening to yourself? I cannot tell the man that I've handed off *all* of the targets to a new hire!"

"You've told him about all my previous training, right?"

"Look. You want me to get more information on the old man. And in order for me to do that, I have to stay on his good side — and for now that means delegating the targets. If I don't, he's going to put someone else in charge. Then where will we be?"

"Brad, look. I'm dealing with things you don't even begin to understand. Know this. Those men cannot under any circumstance be taken out. Period. You've done enough to earn his trust to get to where you are. Use your smarts to find a way around this — *without* letting any of those men get killed. Understand?"

He swore. "Yes. But can't you give me the names of some people who actually need to be killed?"

"This agency doesn't work that way."

"Surely, there are a few names you can drop. That way I can tell Ralf that I've given the assassins targets, and then they can actually—"

"No. Don't call me again unless it's an actual emergency."

The call ended.

He threw his phone across the room. Barely bounced off the wall. No harm. Definitely not broken.

Brad got out of bed and picked it up.

How was he supposed to convince Ralf that he'd passed off the targets when he was doing nothing of the sort?

He needed an answer quickly, because his family's safety depended on it.

Chapter Twenty-Three

BRAD ROSE and stretched his legs. Finally, his last call was almost over.

Without a doubt, this had been the most stressful Saturday he'd had in a while. It even outdid his time in the holding cell. He'd had the chance to take out Ralf, but because he hadn't acted quickly enough, it got interrupted.

A failure.

Now he was back to doing the old man's bidding. Balancing between two opposing bosses. One wrong move, and his family would pay the price.

He should've shot Ralf when he had the chance.

He wouldn't make the same mistake again.

"When does this need to be completed?" Scott asked.

Brad pulled himself from his thoughts and drew a deep breath. "Ralf is on my case about speed, but I'd rather see accuracy. I trust your process. Do what you need to do."

"I don't want to upset Bergmann."

"I'll deal with him. You make sure it's done properly."

They finished their conversation and ended the call. Brad paced the room, guilt stinging for giving each of the assassins bad information. He'd be getting frustrated calls soon enough. And some of them would probably talk to Ralf — so Brad had to find another opportunity to complete his mission ASAP.

For now, he needed to let Ralf know he'd assigned the targets. Then he could rest.

Knock, knock!

He grimaced, wondering what else was needed from him. Clipping the hedges? Mowing the lawn? Driving out of town for some trivial item that somebody needed right away?

Knock, knock!

"You in there, Brad?" Faye called.

"Yeah." He trudged over to the door and opened it.

"Dinner's ready."

"It's already dinnertime?"

"Your mom taught Luna how to make stew."

"Luna's learning to cook?"

"She's having a blast. Come on down. You look like you could use some nourishment." Faye kissed him and headed for the stairs.

Brad stared into the hall for a moment. Maybe she was right, and what he needed was food instead of rest. Or food and then rest. Followed by time to make things right by his dad.

He locked his office and made his way downstairs, the aromas making his mouth water.

Richard sat at the table, next to Mom's normal spot.

Was he now a permanent fixture at the table? One not even worth mentioning, so that Brad could mentally prepare himself for a guest?

Richard rose and extended his hand. "I think we're in for a treat. The food smells delicious."

"That it does." Brad took his seat, which was luckily far

enough away from Richard to make casual conversation challenging with all of the chairs filled.

Richard kept everyone entertained with stories from his days as a forest ranger.

While everyone else laughed and asked questions, it gave Brad a chance to think. His mind had been on overdrive, thanks to the need to come up with the misleading information he'd passed to the other assassins. There was always the chance they'd find the actual information on their own. But it would take time, given what Brad had sent them.

Ralf should be dead and Bancroft should be shutting the whole operation down before they figured out what was going on.

Once the kids started clearing the table, Brad snuck out of the room without anyone noticing.

A hand rested on his arm.

Apparently, someone noticed his stealthy departure.

Richard lifted a brow. "You aren't going to join everyone for the movie?"

He held back a groan. "I didn't realize we were going to gather in the living room after this."

"No, the movie theater."

"Even better."

"You're going to join us, aren't you?" Richard asked.

"I have some work to finish." Brad stepped toward the stairs.

"It would make your mom's day if you went. I think she thought she'd see more of you while staying here."

Brad stopped, irritation building in his chest. "What makes you think you know *my* mother so well? Because you've been playing cards with her for a few days?"

"She does talk to me, about a lot of things." Richard's expression showed no judgment.

That annoyed Brad all the more. "You don't have any idea how much I've done for her. Not just since her injuries, but since my father died. It's been thirty years, and I've been here for my mother that entire time, even as a teenager. I don't know what she's told you."

"All good things, I assure you. I'm just saying that she'd be disappointed if you couldn't make the movie."

All he needed, more guilt. And from Richard, no less.

But if he zoned out during the movie, he could work on his plot against Ralf. And he'd be sitting. That would be restful. He might even be able to get a beer at the theater.

"What do you say?" Richard gave him a friendly smile.

It was impossible to hate this guy.

That made Brad even more frustrated with him.

He drew a deep breath. "After I make a quick call to my boss, I'll be right down."

"Great!" Richard patted his shoulder. "Your mom will be thrilled." He checked the time. "We'll be leaving in twenty minutes."

"Perfect. I'll be ready." Brad raced up the stairs before he could get caught in any more conversation. It was bad enough that he'd gotten talked into going to the movie.

Upstairs, Brad put his phone on speaker to call Ralf as he changed into jeans and hoodie — they always had the AC on in the theater, no matter what time of year it was. And there were really only about two weeks a year when Pine Harbor needed it.

It took several tries before Ralf finally answered. "What's so important?"

"I gave all the assassins the targets."

"Perfect. Do you need anything else?"

"No."

"Great." Ralf ended the call.

Brad shook his head. For as important as Ralf had

made passing off the targets sound, he now acted indifferent.

Whatever. At least Brad had done *his* part.

Both of his bosses should be happy with him.

He stared longingly at his bed.

Now it was time to try and make his family happy. Hopefully, the theater still sold alcohol. It was the only way he'd make it through the evening.

Chapter Twenty-Four

ZEKE STARED ABSENTMINDEDLY at the candy display. It was so lame that he was being forced to come and watch a movie during the HardCorps tournament.

Maybe his family would finally understand the importance after he started earning real money — hundreds of thousands or even millions, like the biggest gamers. But if he kept missing things like this, he'd never reach their level.

When would he finally get a say in his own life? Fifteen? Maybe sixteen, when he got his license. Or would his parents hang onto their power trip until he graduated? It was like they loved calling the shots just because they could.

He would never do that to his kids. He'd actually listen to them. But he'd need to have a girl notice him first. And that prospect seemed light-years away.

"What are you getting, Zeke?" asked Mom.

He brought his attention back to the candy counter and ordered his usual.

Mom turned to Dad. "Are you getting anything, hon?"

Dad looked at the menu. "Where are the beers?"

The guy behind the counter yawned. "Those were discontinued."

"What?" Dad exclaimed. "Since when?"

He shrugged. "A month ago?"

Dad leaned on the counter. "Why?"

"Liability, I think. Not really sure. You gonna get something?"

"That's absurd!"

"Brad, people are staring." Mom looked around. "Just order something."

Dad glared at the cashier. "Next time, I'm sneaking my own in."

The guy shrugged again. "You getting anything?"

Dad grumbled as he shook his head and paid for everyone else's stuff.

Hadley tapped Zeke's shoulder. "What was that about?"

"No idea."

"Dad's really been on edge since I got home."

"Isn't he always?"

"Not like this."

Zeke thought about it. "Yeah, I guess he does seem a little worse than normal."

"A little?"

"Well, yeah. He—" Zeke froze.

Lance and several of his wrestling buddies entered the theater.

Zeke's stomach knotted. He stepped behind Hadley and peeked around her. If Lance saw him, he might make good on his promise to pummel Zeke for tripping him on the bus.

Hadley gave Zeke a funny look. "Now *you're* acting weirder than normal."

"I tripped Lance on the bus, and now he's pissed at me."

"He's captain of the wrestling team, isn't he?"

"How'd you know?"

"Because his older brother is captain of the high school team."

"Even better," Zeke muttered. The two of them could pound him together.

"Why'd you trip him?"

"Because the jerk was throwing things at my head."

"Sometimes you have to let things go. Now look where it got you. You're acting like a scared little mouse because he showed up."

"At least I showed him I won't just take it."

"But now he hates you more than before."

"I don't care."

"You don't?" She tilted her head. "Prove it."

Zeke stepped away from her and watched Lance joking with his friends.

At least he hadn't seen Zeke yet.

Then their gazes met. Locked.

Zeke tried to look away, couldn't. His heart sank.

Lance waved. Gave him an arrogant smirk.

Zeke spun around, his heart pounding.

At least Lance wasn't likely to try anything with Zeke's whole family there. He was safe.

For now.

Hadley poked Zeke. "Grab your stuff."

He took his candy, popcorn, and cherry cola. Kept Lance in his line of sight as his family headed toward the theaters.

Lance waved again.

Zeke swallowed. Lance was plotting his death. That was the only explanation for his boldness. He *wanted*

Zeke to know that he was going to pay for tripping him.

It was only a matter of time. Probably Monday.

That didn't give him much time to prepare. Especially since he had time to make up on the tournament when he got home. Not to mention homework.

Not that homework or the game mattered if he was killed by a wrestler.

"Hurry up." Hadley nudged him. "Lance got you distracted?"

"No."

"Right."

They all piled into theater 12, which was already halfway filled. They had a large group, and there were only a few scattered seats open.

"Looks like we might have to sit separately," Mom said.

Zeke glanced around, hoping Lance wasn't coming in. But then again, he probably wasn't going to watch the feel-good family movie about a kid and his dog.

Luna leaped over to Hadley and grabbed her arm. "I'm with Hadley!"

Richard shook his head. "We can make it work. Where should we sit? Middle? Front?"

"Front!" Luna grinned.

"No." Mom rubbed the back of her neck. "I've already got a crick just thinking about it."

"Middle it is." Richard headed for the stairs.

Dad caught up with him. "Wait. There aren't any rows with enough seats."

"I'm going to ask someone to move."

"What? No, you can't do that."

Richard turned back to him. "Why not?"

"Because … you just can't. It's rude."

"Nonsense." Richard marched over to a row and

started speaking with a guy about Dad's age who was sitting with three kids.

"He's never going to move." Dad covered his face and looked away.

Hadley nudged Zeke. "Look at Dad. He's embarrassed by Richard, just like we always are of him."

Zeke grinned. "You're right. It's kind of fun to watch."

"Right?" She snickered.

He studied her. "You're in a good mood. What's up?"

"What do you mean?"

"I mean, you were so upset you had to go to … uh, you know where." He didn't want to say "mental hospital" with so many people around. "And you weren't exactly happy when you got back."

The corners of her mouth wobbled up and down, and she looked away. "I suppose things look better now. I was miserable when I was away. Now everything seems so much better. Even you." She shoved him.

"Hey!" But he couldn't help laughing.

"Look," Luna said. "Those people are moving for us. Richard did it!"

Sure enough, the family was moving one row down.

Richard turned to Grandma and waved them over.

Dad muttered something unintelligible.

Luna skipped up, nearly spilling her popcorn.

They filed into the row, filling it completely.

Zeke arranged his snacks on the tray while a commercial for a divorce attorney played on the screen. Boring. His mind wandered to Lance, and then to the tournament he was missing. But that was as much of a bummer to think about as Lance, especially when he thought about his troll.

Technically, there were several of them, but it was JimBob who kept creating new logins that worried him.

Every time he thought about it, he kept falling back to the same conclusion.

Wynn.

But that led to an even bigger *why*. Why would his life-long best friend do that to him? Because he was jealous that Zeke could have a channel, and he couldn't? Seemed really lame. Made no sense that he would go to such a low level.

Yet not one of the troll's comments had come in when Wynn was with Zeke. Not that it proved anything. But there was no denying it made Wynn seem more suspicious.

He could always ask Dad if he knew anyone who might be a troll, but that was a big risk. Especially since he was trying to keep up the front that it was no big deal. The last thing he wanted was to worry Dad about the channel.

What if he made Zeke shut everything down?

No way was he going to let that happen.

That meant he needed to ask his friend about it. And it would be tricky. It would offend him, for sure. Might even anger him.

But Zeke needed answers. If they were really friends, they'd work through it.

And yet if Wynn was the troll, everything was over anyway.

Zeke's heart was heavy at the thought of bringing it up. His mouth dried and his pits perspired.

Wynn would be busy with his family for the rest of the weekend. That meant Zeke had until Monday to figure out what to do about Lance and Wynn.

No pressure.

Chapter Twenty-Five

BRAD CHECKED his phone again after pulling into the driveway. No missed calls or texts. He hadn't heard from or seen Ralf all day. And now he was exhausted. Brad was supposed to have had Sunday to relax, but some people at the knife shop had called in sick — hungover was probably more like it — and with nobody else to count on, he had to go in.

It was almost enough to make him wish Kurt was back so he could deal with the long hours and the shop drama.

No. He didn't want that. Just some rest. The less he got, the harder it was to deal with everything.

He got out of the car and looked around. No extra cars parked in front of the house. Good. That meant Richard had gone home where he belonged. Faye and Hadley's cars were also there. Hopefully they were getting rest. Someone should.

Brad stifled a yawn as he set the alarm and started for the walkway.

A car pulled up to the curb.

His stomach twisted. Had to be Richard. Not that it

mattered. Brad was marching straight for his room to catch up on sleep. Everyone else could entertain their guest. Or more like it, he'd keep them laughing.

Brad turned toward the car. It wasn't the Old-Man Mobile that Richard usually drove. It was a matte black sporty sedan with an obnoxiously loud engine. Windows tinted, so he couldn't see who was inside.

The engine didn't turn off. Nobody got out.

Probably a delivery. Seemed like Faye was always ordering something online.

Brad waited, curiosity building despite his fatigue.

The passenger door opened, and out stepped Hadley.

Hadley?

She smiled and waved to the driver. After she closed the door, the car took off.

"Out again?" he asked.

Eyes wide, she turned to him. "Yeah."

"With who?"

She strolled toward the driveway. "Rick."

"Who's that?"

"A guy."

Pain stabbed at his temples. "I guessed that much. Is he from school?"

She shook her head and walked past him.

"Who is he?"

Hadley sighed dramatically and turned around. "He's the guy who helped me at the accident, okay?"

Brad's mind spun. Tried to recall if he'd met him. He hadn't. "You've been keeping in touch with him?"

"Since I got back home, yeah."

"Why?"

"Because he's nice."

"How nice?"

Her shoulders drooped. "Seriously?"

STACY CLAFLIN & NOLON KING

"Yes."

"Are you worried that I'm romantically involved with him?"

"Should I be?"

Hadley shook her head, her brows wrinkling. "Not even close. I'm still getting over Duke."

"How old is he?"

"I don't know."

"Your age? Older?"

"Can we talk about this later?" She threw him an incredulous look. "I mean, really. This isn't a big deal. At all."

"I haven't met him, so it is."

"He's older, but I don't know how much. I haven't asked, because it doesn't matter."

"You're seventeen and living under my roof, so it does matter."

Hadley flipped her hair behind her shoulder. "I'm done talking about this."

"This conversation isn't over!"

"Yes, actually, it is." She spun around and marched toward the door.

"Hadley!"

"Done." She whipped out her key, unlocked the door, and hurried inside, closing it behind her.

Brad shook his head, exhaustion squeezing every inch of his body. He might have to pass this conversation on to Faye. Or at least let it go until he caught up on sleep. Then he could look into Rick later. Hadley was home, safe. For now. That was all that mattered.

He found Faye in the kitchen, helping Luna with some homework. Gave them both a kiss. "If you need anything, I'll be sleeping."

Faye gave him a sad smile. "I'm sorry you haven't been

getting much sleep."

"Just the way it goes. I'll be fine after a good nap." He headed for the hall, but turned back. "What do you know about Rick?"

"Who?"

He grimaced. "Exactly."

"Come again?"

"Rick just dropped off our daughter. Do you know anything about that?"

"Oh, that. She went out for breakfast with a friend."

"Did you know he's older?"

"How much?"

"She wouldn't tell me."

Faye sighed deeply. "I'll see what I can get out of her, but I don't think we should be too hard on her. Not after everything she's been through."

"I'm not saying we have to ground her, but I do need to know more about this man she's spending time with."

"You sure he's a man? Not an older boy?"

"She's seventeen. Anyone older than her is a man."

"He may only be eighteen and in high school. Let's give her some credit."

"Are we talking about the same girl?" He gestured toward the house Duke used to live in, not wanting to say more in front of their youngest.

Faye's mouth formed a straight line. "I'll talk to her after Luna's done with her project."

"I'd appreciate it. See if you can get his last name."

She nodded, but looked doubtful.

Brad trudged upstairs, trying to look into his teenagers' rooms, but both had their doors closed. He didn't have the energy to check in on either of them if it meant a conversation. So he went straight to his room, pulled off his work clothes, and climbed into bed.

It felt like heaven.

He closed his eyes and waited for sleep to take him away.

Instead, thoughts of Rick spun through his mind, worse than a bad psychedelic trip. He tried pushing them away. Faye was going to speak with Hadley, get the guy's last name. Everything would be fine.

But would it?

Hadley's relationship with Duke had nearly destroyed her. Not only had the two-faced predator gotten his teenager pregnant, but his death had landed her in a mental hospital. Not right away, but that had been the impetus.

Was she running to another man to replace the neighbor? Trying to move on or stop thinking about him? And what about her school friends? She never talked about them or had anyone over. Ellie used to be over as much as Wynn was now.

What Hadley needed was to focus on *girl* friends. Even if she didn't return to school, she needed to spend time with them. Or find new friends, if there were issues with the old ones.

He needed to do something to get her focused on them. But it would have to be handled carefully. If she felt like he was pushing, she'd run. She needed to think it was her idea.

Parenting teenagers was so much more complicated. Things were so much simpler when Hadley was Luna's age. He hadn't needed to deal with balancing two bosses back then, either.

Everything had been easier in those days.

Wishing wouldn't change anything. He needed to figure out what to do about his daughter. Soon enough, she'd be out on her own making her own decisions. There was still time for him to protect her, and he was going to do the best he could.

He was an assassin, a trained killer. Why was dealing with one teenage girl so difficult?

Brad bolted upright in bed, eyes wide and pulse racing.

What if this Rick character had been sent by Ralf?

The room felt ten degrees colder.

Ralf had already threatened Brad's family. He might not have meant their *lives*. There were other ways to ruin Brad. And sending an assassin posing as a love interest for his daughter could be his plan.

Brad squeezed the blankets, his breathing growing labored.

His boss could easily set up something like that. Ralf had finally admitted to owning the Slippery Fish. He would've known Hadley was working there. Could've sent someone to follow her other than the guy who was in jail for purposefully causing the accident.

Rick had been there after the accident, ready and eager to help the injured and confused Hadley.

It was too much to be a coincidence.

Ralf had to be behind it. There was no other explanation.

That wasn't true. There was another possible explanation. One potentially less dangerous than one of Ralf's assassins.

Someone from Nate's family could've sent a private investigator to look into the family. Sure, someone was in jail for Nate's disappearance, but that hadn't stopped his birth mother from harassing Faye.

They still believed in Hadley's involvement, despite there being no proof.

He needed to find out who Rick was and what he wanted with Hadley, now more than ever.

Chapter Twenty-Six

FAYE STUDIED HADLEY, seeing so much of her younger self in her oldest child.

"Don't you want me to be happy?" Hadley was on the edge of crying.

"Of course I do. Your dad and I have been doing everything we can to help you."

"Helping me isn't the same as wanting me happy."

"We want you safe *and* happy."

Hadley frowned. "And to control me."

"No. That's not what we want."

"Could've fooled me." Hadley blinked, and a single tear trailed down her face.

Faye drew a deep breath. "Neither Dad nor I have met Rick. You can't blame us for being nervous — especially with you going out alone in his car. Do you really think that's a good idea?"

"I didn't get into his car until I got to know him. I'm not stupid."

"I never said you were. Do you at least understand

where we're coming from? Especially after finding out about how you went behind our backs seeing Duke."

Hadley crossed her arms. "I'm not hiding my *friendship* with Rick."

"What do you do when you get together with him?"

"Just talk. Nothing more."

Faye tilted her head. "I want to believe you."

"Then do! I'm telling you the truth."

"How about this? Next time you get together with him, invite him here. Then we can all meet him."

"No way. Dad will interrogate him, and he'll never want to spend any time with me ever again. Then where will I be? With no friends again. At least now I have one."

"What's wrong with having friends your own age?" Faye asked.

"You'd have to ask *them*. I tried, and it didn't work."

"What ever happened with Ellie?"

Hadley's nostrils flared. "Don't you ever listen to me?"

"Of course I do."

"Then you'd know! I'm not explaining it again."

Faye tried to remember what Hadley said about her best friend. "You need to cut me some slack. This has been the most trying year of my life. On top of being worried sick about you, I've also had to deal with Dad being accused of multiple murders and arrested for one. I also found out that I've been married to an assassin. There's probably more, but it all pales in comparison."

"You forgot to mention Grandma moving in."

"Yes, exactly. In light of all that, would you do me the favor of refreshing my memory about Ellie?"

Hadley's eyes narrowed. "She turned against me. Probably never was a real friend to begin with — just wanted to hang out with me to be popular. Now she's got everything at school that I did, and has turned everyone against me so I wouldn't be in her way. Happy?"

Faye's breath hitched. "No. That's awful. Is that why you don't want to go to school?"

"You think?"

"No need to be sarcastic. I'm only trying to help."

"Whatever." Hadley looked away.

Faye bit her tongue. It would take every ounce of her self-control to remain calm in the face of so much teenage attitude. "What about Lucy? You were spending time with her before the accident, weren't you? Plus, didn't you say she'd visited you in the hospital?"

Hadley nodded, still turned away from Faye.

"Have you seen her since you got back?"

Hadley shook her head.

"Does she know you're back?"

Hadley shrugged.

"Has your voice box stopped working?"

She turned to Faye, her brows furrowing. "Would you leave me alone? I'm tired of talking about this."

"This is important."

"Rick is good for my mental health. Can't that be enough? I'm going to be eighteen soon, and you guys need to get used to me making my own decisions. What do you think is going to happen after I graduate? That you're going to keep telling me what to do?"

"We aren't trying to order you around now."

Hadley snorted. "Right."

"We *aren't*."

This conversation was going nowhere, and fast. It would probably be better if they both had some space.

Faye put her hand on her daughter's arm. "Just know that Dad and I love you very much, and we're trying to look out for you."

Hadley didn't respond.

"We're both tired. Why don't we sleep on it, and talk tomorrow? Think about inviting Rick over. Dad and I would really like to meet him." It took a lot of effort to keep her tone even. She wanted to yell and make demands, but that would only push Hadley away further.

"Fine. I'll think about it."

"Thank you." Faye forced a smile and kissed the top of Hadley's head before going out into the hall and closing the door between them.

She'd forgotten to ask Rick's last name.

Brad was going to be pissed.

He'd have to get over it. She was doing the best she could, and he knew how impossible their daughter was being. That was why he'd asked her to deal with Hadley.

And now her heart and mind were both racing.

Faye looked for Brad in their room. Empty. But the light was on underneath his office door.

Probably best they didn't talk right now. The last thing she felt like doing was telling him she hadn't gotten Rick's last name. Maybe she could ask Hadley in passing before seeing Brad.

She needed some air.

Faye checked on Luna, who was assembling a puzzle with Dianne. Then she grabbed her coat and headed outside. Stars twinkled in the dark, clear canopy overhead.

The perfect setting for calming her nerves. Frogs even croaked in the distance.

She took in the crisp, fresh night air and stepped onto the sidewalk, heading nowhere in particular. Images of the neighbors gathered in front of Duke's old house filled her mind. Everyone had been so shocked to find out about his death. And then Allison's. Now Nate was gone, and most everyone rightly assumed he was dead. If Brad was right

— and their family's security depended on it — the neighbors would never learn of the proof. The fall guy would remain behind bars.

Faye strolled along, stopping every so often to think about the people living inside the houses — or the people who *had* lived in them. The home that brought her the most sadness was the Campbells' old house. Now it had a *For Sale* sign out front. The price had already been lowered several times.

Too many people knew the history: Allison's murder at her husband's hand. Only a rare few knew he had been an assassin in addition to being a murderer, that he'd been involved with Duke's killing, too.

Yes, this house would be an even more challenging sale than Duke's had been. At least a killer hadn't resided there.

The Campbells' lawn was too long and the bushes were in desperate need of a trim. Allison would've hated to see it like that.

"Sad, isn't it?"

Faye whipped around, pulse drumming in her ears.

Paula stood there, mouth contorted.

Faye regained her composure. "Yes, horribly so."

"My baby spent most of his life within those walls. I never should've given him up. Then he'd still be alive."

"People still say he got away."

Paula's brows furrowed. "The man accused of kidnapping him *claims* Nate is still alive."

"Then there's hope."

"Have you spoken with your daughter about Nate?" Paula stepped closer.

Faye inched away. "She's innocent."

"You sure about that?"

"My daughter would never want to hurt anyone. She cried when she found a mouse in a trap." Sure, she'd been nine, but that was beside the point. "Excuse me. I need to get going."

Paula stepped in front of her. "Why were you looking at the Campbells' house?"

"Not that I need to explain myself to you, but I'm on a walk and didn't even realize I'd stopped. Allison was my friend, and I find everything the family has gone through to be nothing short of tragic."

"Can't argue with that."

Faye stepped around her. "I'll see you around."

Paula leaped in front of her and grabbed her arms. "You need to let me talk with Hadley."

"Get your hands off me!" Faye shook her arms and moved back.

The woman had a tight grip. "I have to talk to her!"

Faye finally yanked herself free. "No, you do not."

"She knows *something*! You may not be able to see it, because you're her mother. I get that. It's hard for me to think about Nate ever having done wrong. But I'm willing to believe it if that'll point to the truth, to where he is."

"You need to leave me and my family alone. Your behavior is bordering on harassment. I'd prefer not getting our lawyer involved, but if I have to I will."

Paula squeezed Faye's shoulders and shook her, only an inch from her face. "I need to know what she's hiding!"

Faye shoved her, but she didn't let go. "Stop! You're hurting me."

"Your lies are hurting me!" Spittle landed on Faye's face.

Anger raced through her. She made a fist, maneuvered between Paula's arms, and punched her.

The other woman gasped and stepped away. "You just hit me!"

"You wouldn't let go of me, and you were threatening me."

Paula furrowed her brows. "I'm calling the police!"

"I hope you're ready to be arrested, because you assaulted me first. I was trying to get away from you, and I had no other choice but to act in self-defense."

"*I* was acting in self-defense! You're hiding information that could help me find my son. What else was I supposed to do?"

"How about, not grabbing me?" Faye glowered at her and stepped back. "That would be a great place to start."

Paula fell onto the overgrown grass, tears streaming down her face. "All I want is to find my boy! I've never had a chance to meet him. I just want to find him. Do you know how that feels?"

Faye rubbed her sore shoulder. "No, and I feel for you. I do. But my daughter can't tell you where Nate is because she doesn't know."

At least in saying that, Faye was able to offer the desperate mom the truth. Hadley didn't know where Nate's body was. She vaguely knew it was in the harbor, but that was the extent of it.

Paula buried her face in her hands and said something Faye couldn't make out.

Sighing, Faye sat next to her, leaving plenty of space between them. "I didn't catch that."

Paula glance at her, eyes widening in surprise. Probably figured Faye would've run off given the chance.

That would've been the smart thing to do, but Faye couldn't leave her sitting there in tears in the Campbells' now-overgrown yard, even though they'd just had words and a scuffle.

"I can't stand the thought that I might never meet him." Paula wiped her eyes and sniffled. "In my mind, I always pictured a heartwarming meet-up once he was an adult. What if that never happens?"

Guilt stung. Faye knew it never could happen, but she would take that secret to the grave.

"I guess I'll have to move on, but it won't be easy. And I don't think I can ever give up. What am I supposed to do?"

Faye chose her words carefully. "Anyone in your position would be devastated — losing a child is a kind of trauma. Have you talked with someone?"

"Of course I have."

"I mean a therapist. I go once a week, and it's helped so much."

Paula sniffled. "What did it help you with?"

Faye was taken aback. It wasn't something she wanted to share with a stranger, but if it would send Paula back to wherever she came from she would be happy to tell her something. It wasn't like they talked about killing in therapy.

Paula looked at her expectantly.

"Mostly childhood stuff," Faye spit out. "Daddy issues."

"I have those, too." Paula sniffled again.

Faye dug into her pocket and handed her a pack of tissues.

"Thanks." Paula yanked one out. "I imagine if I'd raised Nate, I'd probably carry these around with me."

"Comes with the territory."

Paula blew her nose and turned back to Faye. "I'm sorry for going after you like I did. I don't know what I was thinking."

Faye thought back to the night she and Brad dumped Nate's body into the harbor. "We all do things we normally wouldn't when we're desperate."

Chapter Twenty-Seven

BRAD PUT DOWN THE PHONE, nearly ready to drive over to Ralf's house. Not that it would do much good if the man was ignoring him. He could just as easily not answer the door as not answer the phone.

He yawned and checked the time. It was getting late. Might as well head to bed and get what rest he could. Maybe he could take some time off from the knife shop. It wasn't like Kurt hadn't done that plenty of times.

Tuesdays were notoriously slow. Tomorrow, he'd find someone who had missed today and temporarily put them in charge.

Perfect plan. If Ralf was still avoiding him, there was nothing he could do about it.

Brad closed his laptop, turned off the lights, and locked his office door. The hall was dim, and no light shone from under Zeke's door. No light under Hadley's door, either.

He went to his room and found it empty. Had Faye mentioned that she was going somewhere? She was probably downstairs, getting the salon ready for the week.

By the time he got out of the shower, she was in bed reading.

He gave her a kiss. "I was wondering where you disappeared to."

Was it his imagination, or did her face flush with a little color?

She put her book down. "I just needed some air after talking with Hadley."

"Makes sense. Did you find out anything else about Rick?"

"Not a lot, and I didn't get his last name yet."

"We'll both keep trying. Besides, there can't be that many of them." Brad sat and rubbed her shoulders.

She grimaced and squirmed away from him.

"What's the matter?"

"Nothing."

"That wasn't nothing."

"I'm just sore." She didn't come closer.

He studied her. "What happened?"

"It's late, and I have an early client. I need to get some sleep."

"Faye, what's wrong?"

"Nothing."

"I don't buy that when Hadley says it either."

She released a long, slow breath before making eye contact with him. "I've been having issues with Nate's birth mom, but they're resolved now."

"Resolved?"

"Paula showed up again while I was getting air a little bit ago. We had words. Then it got physical."

"Physical?" Heat rose in Brad's chest. "Meaning what, exactly?"

Faye looked away. "She grabbed me. I punched her."

"You punched her?" Admiration ran through him.

"Not my best moment, but what other choice did I have? She wouldn't let go, even when I told her to."

"I'm not judging. I'm impressed."

She turned to him. "You are?"

"Yes. I'm proud of you for doing what was needed. You're always saying violence isn't the answer, but sometimes it is."

Faye frowned.

"I know you *wish* it wasn't," Brad added, "but that's the world we live in."

"Not the world I want for our kids."

"But it's still where we live."

She sighed.

"Are you okay?" He scooted closer. "Did she hurt your shoulders?"

"She grabbed me and squeezed, and wouldn't let go. I'm sure she's sorer than I am. Probably going to have a black eye."

Brad held up a hand for a high-five.

Faye looked at him like he was crazy.

"Don't leave me hanging."

"I'm not proud of what I did. She could've called the cops, you know. She even threatened to."

"But she didn't?"

Faye shook her head.

"Because she knew she was in the wrong." He nudged his hand closer to Faye.

She gave him a pathetic high-five.

"That's better. Now let me see your shoulders."

"Like I said, it's nothing."

"And like I said, let me see."

"You're annoying, you know that?"

"Only because I care."

The corners of her mouth curved up slightly, and she scooted closer.

He undid the top buttons of her nightshirt and looked at her shoulder. Bruises in the shapes of fingers.

"Nate's mom did this?"

"She apologized, then we had a decent talk. She's going to leave us alone."

"You sure about that?"

Faye started to cover the bruises, but he stopped her and grabbed his phone from the nightstand to take pictures — first one shoulder, then the other.

"What are you doing?" she asked.

"Collecting evidence. In case we need to file for a restraining order."

"It won't be a problem." Faye fixed her buttons. "She said she was going home."

"People don't always do what they say. What if she comes back?"

"I suppose I'll have to punch her again."

"Good."

"Not really."

Brad kissed her cheek and climbed into his side of the bed. "If she doesn't leave, let me know right away."

"What are you going to do? Punch her?"

"I'm not a barbarian."

Her mouth fell open.

Brad laughed. "I'm teasing. But seriously, we'll need to file a report."

"Like the police will take us seriously."

"That's what the pictures are for."

"I believed her when she said she would go back home."

"As long as she leaves you alone, I don't care what she does."

They talked about Hadley for a few minutes before turning out the light. Brad fell asleep as soon as the room went dark.

When his alarm went off, Faye was already gone. She hadn't been kidding about the early appointment.

Before he could finish getting dressed, Bancroft called.

He answered, yawning. "Brad here."

"You sleeping?" she asked.

"I don't talk in my sleep. What do you need?"

"Have you gotten any new information from Ralf?"

"The man won't answer my calls."

"Why not?"

"If you manage to get ahold of him, you'll have to ask yourself."

"Funny." She didn't sound amused. "You need to reach him."

"I'm doing my best. Never been trained, remember? I'm just a regular guy you pulled from a holding cell."

"You're no regular guy. What did you end up doing about the targets Ralf's so anxious to take out?"

"I gave bad information to my assassins. They're not going to find the targets, much less kill them. At least not any time soon."

"You sure about that?"

"Yes."

"You'd better be right."

"I am."

"Keep the wire on you at all times. We're getting close. The things you got out of him on Saturday were good. We need more of that."

"If he'll talk to me."

"Find a way. Or wait until you're sure he's not home and get that code book the old-fashioned way."

The call ended.

Brad muttered, but donned the wire even though it was probably useless. Made sure it was off. Didn't want the agent listening in on his conversations at home.

He knocked on Hadley's door, but got no response. Probably sleeping in, or maybe doing an online class — he had no idea if those were live.

Downstairs, Faye sat at the kitchen table with a coffee. "Good morning."

"That's yet to be seen." He yawned, kissed her, and filled a travel mug for himself. "Already drop Mom off at the center?"

"Richard picked her up."

Brad nearly dropped his drink. "What?"

"He offered."

"I could've taken her, if it wasn't convenient for you."

"He offered, and she accepted. I had nothing to do with the matter."

Brad frowned. "Nobody asked me."

"You have to let your mom grow up sometime." Faye smiled at him.

He resisted the urge to tell her his fear that Ralf had sent Richard to get close to his mother, in case he needed a hostage. But he had no proof, and Faye didn't need yet another reason to worry herself sick.

"He's a good guy. She's been so much happier since she met him."

"If you say so."

"I do." She put her mug in the sink and kissed him. "Gotta run. Just heard a car pull up. Must be my next client."

"Is Richard dropping Mom off this evening, too?"

"Not sure." Faye hurried into the hallway.

Brad collapsed onto a chair and took a big swig of coffee. His mom even had boyfriend. It wasn't that he didn't want her happy, but it had been so long since she'd dated. What if she got herself into trouble?

His phone rang.

Ralf.

His breath caught in his throat. He fumbled with the wire to turn it on and managed to answer the phone before it went to voicemail. Put it on speaker.

"Brad here."

"None of the targets are dead yet, Morris!" Ralf shouted. "Can you explain that?"

At least he didn't have to worry about Bancroft not being able to hear.

"I'm heading into the shop now," Brad said. "I'm going to speak with them as soon as—"

"Don't bother!"

"Excuse me?"

"Stay home, Morris. I'm demoting you."

His heart plummeted. "What?"

"You heard me."

The call ended.

Brad swore.

His phone rang.

Bancroft.

He swore again.

Chapter Twenty-Eight

ZEKE'S HEART pounded harder with every passing moment. By the time the bus stopped in front of school, his hands were shaking.

Lance would be waiting for him. Not only that, he needed to ask Wynn if he was the troll.

It was going to be a crappy day. Maybe he'd be better off not confronting Wynn. Lance was a big enough problem for one day. Besides, he could use Wynn's help with the bully.

Yeah, that was a good idea. He would talk to Wynn another day.

Luckily, his friend talked through the ride. Didn't even notice how quiet Zeke was being. He was too focused on how pushy and obnoxious his dad's girlfriend had been all weekend, telling Zeke every detail.

"You listening to me?" Wynn asked, as they stepped off the bus.

It was like his friend could read his mind.

Zeke turned to him. "Yeah, of course."

"Then what did I say?"

"Your dad's girlfriend is crazy."

"That goes without saying — because that's *not* what I just said."

Zeke sighed. "Fine, you got me. But today's my last on this earth, so I think that's a good excuse."

"What are you talking about?"

"Lance. Remember? He waved at me at the movie theater."

"Oh yeah." Wynn looked chagrined. "You gonna fight or run?"

Zeke sighed. "I don't know. Just want to avoid him. Maybe he's home sick today."

Wynn looked around. "I don't see him."

"Just means he isn't *here*. Doesn't mean he isn't at school." They went through the front doors, into the noisy main hall.

Zeke's stomach lurched. Lance was probably ready to pummel him, and had brought his wrestling friends in on it, too.

It would be the whole team against him.

Definitely his last day alive.

Wynn put his arm around Zeke. "I've got your back. And if it makes you feel better, I can talk to Trey and Sal."

"From the chess team?" Zeke exclaimed. "What good are they going to be?"

"They can help me back you up."

Zeke groaned. "I should've stayed home sick."

"Can't do that forever."

"No, but I'd have a full extra day to think about what to do."

"May as well just face him now. Get it over with."

Zeke started to say something, but the warning bell rang.

"See you later!" Wynn ran off.

Leaving Zeke alone.

He resisted the urge to let his shoulders slump — he didn't have to *look* like the wimp he felt like.

A couple girls giggled off to the right. Probably at him.

Even so, he looked. One of the girls, a short brunette with curls, smiled at him.

He looked behind him.

Nobody else.

He turned back to the girl.

She waved before catching up with her friends.

Zeke blinked a few times. He had to have imagined that. But looking behind him again revealed that there was nobody else the girl could've been smiling and waving at.

Not that there was any time to ponder that. He bolted down the hallway, making it to his seat just as the final bell rang. The teacher rambled on, but all Zeke could think about was Lance, and how he was going to destroy Zeke's face.

Once that class ended, Zeke hurried to his next one, keeping an eye out for the wrestler.

So far, so good.

But lunch was the period he was most concerned about. He and Lance ate at the same time.

The rest of his morning classes both dragged and flew by at the same time. Dragged on because he couldn't focus, and flew by because he didn't want his life to end.

But it was inevitable.

Zeke grabbed his food and sat at a table with other gaming nerds before Wynn could drag him to a table full of chess players.

He picked at his food and watched the clock when he wasn't looking around for Lance. He and his friends were usually too cool to eat in the cafeteria, so it wasn't surprising that they were nowhere in sight.

That meant Zeke would be staying there until the bell rang. Safely.

At least until after school. That was when the big fights usually happened.

He had a couple more hours before his death. And he had to spend them in class.

Lame.

He really should've stayed home sick. Given the way his stomach felt, it wasn't a lie.

There was no way he could sit through two more hours of classes.

It was now or never.

Zeke rose, nearly knocking over his chair.

"You okay?" Wynn asked.

"No. I'm going to find Lance."

Wynn's mouth dropped open. "Now?"

"Yes. I'm done waiting."

A chorus of whispers went around the table.

The tray shook in his hands. He took a deep breath and marched toward the garbage cans. Threw away his trash. Took another deep breath and opened the door to the hallway.

Do or die.

The door didn't close behind him like it should.

He whipped around.

Everyone from his table stood behind him.

Zeke swallowed. "What are you doing?"

Wynn cracked his knuckles. "Backing you up."

"You are?" Zeke stared at the group in disbelief as they all nodded.

"Let's do this." Wynn stepped up next to Zeke and looked around. "Now, if I was a cocky wrestler, where would I be?"

A kid stopped walking and turned to Wynn. "You looking for Lance?"

"That obvious, huh?"

"He and some of the other wrestlers are out in the courtyard kicking around a hacky sack."

"Thanks, man." Wynn strutted toward the courtyard.

Zeke's insides turned to mush. He feet wouldn't budge.

This was stupidest decision of his life.

Wynn glanced back. "Come on. What are you waiting for?"

"Yeah," agreed the other kids.

Zeke looked around, gaining a little confidence from the group. "Let's go."

His heart beat hard and his stomach tingled, but at least he wasn't alone. At least as long as the other kids didn't jump ship once they saw Lance.

Then Wynn opened the door to the courtyard.

Zeke nearly lost his lunch.

The other kids urged him on.

His mind spun, but he managed to get his feet moving. Found himself marching straight for Lance, who was too busy laughing at one of his friends to notice him.

Zeke waited until Lance turned his way. "I believe we have something to discuss."

The wrestler jolted, raked his fingers through his hair.

Zeke noticed he actually stood taller than Lance. He did have an advantage. Not to mention the kids behind him.

"What do you want?" Lance scowled. "Gonna trip me again?"

"Depends. You gonna throw things at my head again?"

Some of the wrestlers laughed.

Lance tilted his head dramatically. "You gonna keep being such a loser?"

"Are you going to keep thinking you're better than everyone else?"

"Yeah, because I *am*." He waggled his tongue. "Whatcha gonna do about it? Loser."

Anger boiled in Zeke's chest.

He started to say something, but then the short girl from that morning stepped up. "You have no idea who you're talking to."

Lance burst out laughing. "You mean, Mr. Stuck in the Eighties. Yeah, I know exactly who he is."

She crossed her arms and narrowed her eyes. "If he's so stuck in eighties, then why does he have over ten thousand followers on his YouTube channel?"

"What's the channel about? How to be a number one loser?" Lance burst out laughing and punched one the other wrestlers, who then joined the laughter.

"He's one of the top HardCorps players."

Heat crept into Zeke's face. "I wouldn't say *top* players."

Lance glanced at him. "Shut up. I wanna hear what your little girlfriend has to say."

She stepped closer. "My name's Olive. And I'm not his girlfriend." She glanced at Zeke before turning back to Lance. "I'm his biggest fan. He doesn't know me."

Wynn nudged Zeke. "You need to get to know that girl."

That went without saying.

Lance turned to Zeke. "This true?"

Zeke swallowed and then stood taller, a fire raging in his chest. "Yeah. What's it to you?"

Wynn snickered.

Lance's brows drew together. "I mean about the channel. People actually follow you? People other than your mom?"

"She doesn't follow me."

Chuckles sounded behind Lance.

He pulled out his phone. "I need to see this see this for myself. What's your username?"

"ZombieKiller86."

"Like I said, obsessed with the eighties." Lance's finger flew around his screen.

Wynn gave Zeke a hopeful look.

Maybe this wasn't going to end badly after all.

He looked around. The small crowd had doubled, and more were coming in through the doors. His pulse drummed in his ears. The people had to be Lance's friends, because they surely weren't Zeke's.

Wynn tried to look at Lance's phone. "Well?"

The wrestler's mouth contorted and he turned to Zeke. "This is really you?"

"Look at the profile picture." Zeke glanced nervously at the doors, where even more kids were coming outside to watch.

Lance looked back and forth between Zeke and his screen. "You have even more followers than the chick said."

"My name is Olive." She glared at Lance.

Zeke grinned at her spunk.

She smiled at him.

His face flushed with heat.

One of Lance's friends nudged him. "Look. His count is growing fast."

"I just followed him!" said a voice in the crowd.

"Me too!"

"And me!"

Several others joined in.

Zeke looked around in disbelief as others admitted to following him.

His confidence grew, and he made eye contact with Lance. "You going to leave me alone now? Stop throwing things at me? Stop making fun of me?"

Olive stood next to him. "If you don't, you'll have to deal with me."

Lance looked down at her. "You think that's supposed to worry me?"

"I have a red belt in Tae Kwon Do. You wouldn't know what hit you."

Wynn stepped up. "And you'll have to go through me, too."

The other kids from the lunch table said the same thing.

So did some other people Zeke didn't even know.

Lance looked at all of them, his face paling.

"What do you have to say now?" Zeke demanded.

"Just don't trip me again." Lance glared at him before stalking away.

Zeke's knees turned to rubber.

Olive turned to him. "Are you going to the dance with anyone on Saturday?"

"There's a HardCorps event that day."

Wynn shoved him.

"Uh, I mean no. I'm not going with anyone." Zeke cleared his throat, and he was sure his knees would give out. "Do you want to go with me?"

"You bet I do. Let's trade digits."

"Okay." Zeke fumbled for his phone.

Pinched himself. He was awake. This was all really happening.

Chapter Twenty-Nine

HADLEY TOOK in a deep breath of the salty harbor air mixed with the aromas of fried foods. Took in the sounds of shouts from the carnival games and shrieks from kids. She felt a rush of nostalgia — back in middle school, she'd looked forward to this all year.

The Pine Harbor Fish Festival was always the signal of warmer days ahead, a reminder of the impending summer vacation. It had always been one of the highlights of every year, and now it felt like a sign of good things to come. The new beginning that she so desperately wanted.

She'd never missed a year, even when she'd gotten sick with the flu at the age of twelve and she'd managed to get better just in time to attend on the last day. Last year, she'd gone twice. Once with her family and another time with Duke, sneaking away from school and skipping a rehearsal.

It had been so worth it. She and Duke had fed each other corndogs and sauerkraut pizza before kissing at the top of the Ferris wheel. That was the best selfie ever. She'd wanted to frame it and put it in her room, but she didn't want to have to explain any of it to her parents.

"You ready?" Rick's voice brought Hadley back to the present. He held up the two neon green wristbands that would get them on any ride they wanted for the whole day.

"Yeah." She took one of the bands and adjusted it so that it fit over her hand.

"Where do you want to start?" Rick looked toward the Ferris wheel.

"How about a game?" Hadley gestured toward some oddly-shaped dartboards. She'd decided she wouldn't get sad today no matter what. Any memories of Duke would only be good. If something was too much, she'd simply avoid it.

This was about having a fresh start.

"Sounds like fun." He grinned at her, reached for her hand, but then pulled away. "Let's go."

She walked alongside him, a mixture of guilt and relief coursing through her. Part of her wanted to hold Rick's hand — new beginnings — but she also didn't know if it was too soon.

How long exactly was a seventeen-year-old supposed to wait after her boyfriend's death before she opened her heart up to someone else? It wasn't like there was a rulebook for this sort of thing. What would Duke have thought?

She didn't have much time to ponder it, as she and Rick start throwing darts — most of which didn't even stick to the board.

"These are rigged," Rick muttered.

Just what Duke would've said. Probably had.

Hadley flipped her hair back and smiled. "Aren't they all?"

They played more games before snacking on deep-fried coffee- and chocolate-covered pork rinds.

"Don't you wish we could eat these year round?" Rick grimaced as he finished his off.

She laughed. "Once a year is enough for me."

"Do you want to try a ride?"

Hadley flashed back to throwing up on one of the rollercoasters a few years back. "Not after this food. Let's check out some of the fish booths and let our stomachs settle."

"Sounds like a plan." He gave her a sweet smile and helped her from the chair. But he didn't keep hold of her hand.

More disappointment and guilt. Though it was probably a good thing that he was such a gentleman. She did need the time to figure out what she needed. What Duke would think if he could see her now. He wouldn't have wanted her to be miserable. But would he want her to mourn him longer?

Would he feel insulted or honored that Rick reminded her of him?

Once they were ready to head for the rides, he turned to her and paused. Chewed on his lip and took a deep breath.

Her heart skipped a beat. This seemed like a serious moment. What was he going to say? Did she want to know?

She cleared her throat. "Is everything okay?"

"I really like spending time with you."

Her stomach knotted. "I sense a 'but' coming."

Rick frowned.

"I knew it. What is it?"

"Not a 'but' exactly. Though there is something I need to tell you."

A lump formed in her throat, she struggled to breathe normally. "What?"

"I'm—" His phone rang. "I have to take this."

Of course he did.

She nodded and stepped away, watching as he answered and turned his back to her.

Her stomach twisted, and it wasn't from the carnival food. What was he going to tell her? Why now? And why here, with so many people around?

He had to be concerned about her reaction.

Trying to swallow back the lump in her throat, she imagined what he needed to tell her. Had he been sent by Dad's boss, like her father had worried about? Was he married? Divorced with a kid? Something much worse?

Rick came over, his face stormy. "I'm sorry, but I've been called in for work. I can't get out of it."

"Now?" she exclaimed.

"I tried to get out of it." He drew in a deep breath. "Can I walk you to your car? Or do you want to stay?"

Her shoulders slumped. "Can you come back later? These wristbands are good until closing."

"Maybe." He looked deep in thought. "I could call you."

Hadley's heart pounded. "Can you at least tell me what you were going to say?"

He glanced at the time and then held her hand in his. "Not like I need to. It's an emergency, and I have to go now. I promise I'll tell you as soon as I can."

She sighed.

"Do you want me to walk you to your car, or are you going to stay?"

The last thing she wanted was to go home and face anyone in her family. "I'm going to stay — at least for a little while."

"Understood." He squeezed her hand before letting go. "I'll let you know how long I think it'll be once I get there. We can always come back. The festival is all week."

She nodded. "And you'll tell me what you were going to say?"

"I promise." He turned around and bolted away.

Hadley stared until he was out of sight.

Now what was she supposed to do? Go on rides by herself? Didn't get much more lame than that.

"Hadley?"

She spun around. "Lucy?"

Her friend threw her arms around her. "It's so good to see you! Feels like it's been forever. How's virtual school?"

Hadley gave her a quick squeeze before standing back. "It's okay. I mean, school is school."

"So true. But you can do it all in your pajamas, right?"

"Kind of." Hadley shrugged. "I have to be on video, so I have to be presentable from my shoulders up."

"I'd totally wear PJ pants all day."

Hadley tried to hide a smile. "I usually do. How's school? Did you guys already perform the play?"

"Yeah. This week is tryouts for the next one. You should totally do it. Virtual school kids are allowed to participate — I asked."

"You did?"

Lucy nodded. "The last play wasn't the same without you."

"I—" A part of Hadley wanted to go back, to be center stage once again. "I can't."

"Why not?"

She looked away. "Everyone hates me."

"What? No they don't."

"Ellie does. Most everyone from the drama club follows her lead."

"Ellie's had a change of heart."

"I'd have to see that to believe it."

"She has, I'm serious."

"What happened?" Hadley frowned.

"I think she feels bad."

"About what?"

"The way she treated you."

"Funny." Hadley laughed bitterly. "She hasn't said anything to me about it. It isn't like she doesn't know my number or where I live."

"Maybe you could reach out to her?"

Hadley stood up straight, indignant. "Me, go to her? You've got to be kidding. I know you don't know everything that happened between us, but she said some pretty awful stuff. If she thinks *I'm* going to crawl back to her, she's lost her mind."

Lucy's expression softened. "I don't think it's like that."

"What, then?"

"More like she knows how much she hurt you, and she's worried about your reaction."

Hadley snorted. "*She's* worried about what I'll think? That's rich."

"She wants to make up with you."

"And how would you know?"

Lucy stepped a little closer. "Promise you won't say I told you?"

"Sure."

"I'm serious."

"Fine, I won't say anything." Hadley waited for Lucy to continue. "I promise. Want me to pinky swear?"

Lucy shook her head, the corners of her mouth twitching. "No. She's been talking about you a lot to me."

"Did she tell you all about Duke?"

Lucy arched a brow. "She's been asking me how you

are and if you've said anything about her to me. She wants to talk to you, but only if she knows you aren't mad."

Hadley drew in a deep breath.

"Are you?"

"Yes, of course. But if she apologizes, and means it, we can probably move on."

"You really mean that?" Lucy's eyes lit up.

"I don't see why we can't get past it — if she's really sorry. We *have* been best friends for a long time."

"Great!" Lucy grabbed Hadley's hand. "Let's go talk to her now."

Hadley yanked her hand away. "Right now?"

"Yeah. They're over there eating." Lucy pointed to where she'd eaten with Rick not long before.

"I don't know."

"Why not?"

Hadley backed away, shaking her head. "No. Tell her to call me, or stop by."

"Wait—"

Hadley ran off, hiding in the crowd until she lost sight of Lucy.

She should've stayed in bed.

Chapter Thirty

BRAD CLOSED his laptop and looked around the coffee shop. Everyone else definitely looked happier than him. He'd been there all day because he wasn't going back to BlueBlade as an underling again. And he sure didn't feel like telling Faye about his demotion. She'd want to know what it meant.

He had no idea.

Brad had spent most of the morning fuming behind his computer, ingesting an unreal amount of caffeine. Then he'd spent most of the afternoon trying to reach his boss. Not surprisingly, Ralf wasn't answering calls, texts, or emails.

His phone rang.

Brad whipped it out.

It was Bancroft.

"Brad here."

"Make any progress yet?"

"I can't reach him."

"You have to do something. Go to his house."

"Haven't we been through this before? He's refusing contact with me, so that means he won't answer the door."

"Give him a reason to open it."

Brad sighed. "Like what? Throw eggs at it?"

She didn't laugh. "You know the man. What would get him to let you in?"

There was one thing, but the agent wouldn't like it. Not one bit. If he was going to do that, he couldn't let her in on it.

"Well?" she demanded.

"I'll think of something."

"You'd better. I'm calling in an hour."

"An hour?" he exclaimed.

"That's what I said." She ended the call.

He had sixty minutes to get his job back. And his boss was unreachable.

No problem.

Muttering under his breath, he gathered his things and made his way to his car. Checked to make sure he had his weapons. The gun and knife were both in the car. Tucked them into his pockets. He hadn't brought the wire; it was still tucked into another belt. He did, however, have the agent's wire.

That wouldn't be on him, either.

If he was able to have a conversation with Ralf, Bancroft couldn't hear it. She would freak out.

But she wanted him to get back in his boss's good grace. So she would have to deal with Brad doing things his way.

He called Ralf.

Voicemail, as expected.

"This is Brad. I know you're busy, but we need to talk. I have a proposal for you, and it's something you won't want to refuse. We'll talk in fifteen."

He set the phone down and started driving. It would take most of that time to get to the mansion. He glanced at the screen every so often to see if Ralf got back to him.

Nothing.

Everything rode on Ralf answering the door.

When Brad pulled up to his boss's house, the Bentley was in the driveway.

At least he knew the old man was home.

He would ring the doorbell until he was let in. Or until the cops showed up. He wasn't going back to the holding cell over this.

Brad checked his gun and knife, making sure they were securely in place, before getting out of the car. He marched up to the front door as if Ralf had invited him over for a scotch.

Knocked three times.

Then again.

Waited. Looked up and down the street.

Rang the doorbell.

Texted Ralf. Called him.

Leaned against the wall and caught up on some missed texts from other people. Faye wanted to know if he'd be home around the normal time. Some of the assassins had questions about their targets — obviously they hadn't gotten the memo about Brad's demotion.

He sent each some more false information, to send them in the wrong direction.

Rang the doorbell again.

Pressed his face against the window, though it was frosted to make it impossible to see in. Brad was sure Ralf would be able to see him if he was within range.

A dead bolt clicked.

Brad forced back a smile and pulled away from the window.

Ralf stood there, looking as if he'd just sucked on a lemon. "Can I help you?"

"So glad I finally reached you. Did you get my message?" He stepped forward, but his boss didn't move aside.

"Which one?"

"Good point. I did leave more than one, didn't I?"

"You could say that."

"Let's go in and discuss."

Ralf's brows drew together. "What makes you think I'm letting you inside?"

"Because I have a proposition for you."

"Do you not know the meaning of the word demoted?"

"The sooner you let me in, the sooner I can get going."

Ralf scowled.

"Or we could stand here all night. That works, too. I'm in no hurry."

"What is this involving?"

"I can guarantee that all your targets will be taken out quickly."

"Define quick."

Brad faked a shiver. "It's getting cold out here. Let's step inside."

"I *am* inside."

Brad stared Ralf down. "Look, we both know what you want is for these targets to be taken care of. The faster the better. I can make that happen."

"You already proved you can't."

"That's where you're wrong."

Ralf lifted a brow. "In other words, you want a second chance."

"If you'll allow me to prove myself, you won't be disappointed."

Ralf looked at his Rolex. "You have until tomorrow, end of day."

Ralf slammed the door shut.

Brad stepped back. He had roughly twenty-four hours to make more than a dozen hits happen?

That was insanity.

But it was better than nothing. It would certainly piss off the agent, but surely she could fake the death of at least one of the men. She'd done it before, to divert Kurt's attention. Why not do it again, now that everything was on the line?

She'd wanted Brad to get his position back. He had. Now she could deal with the consequences of the way he'd done it.

Once his boss believed one of the targets dead, that should give Brad the chance to demand another meeting.

Then he would make his move.

He called the agent, put it on speaker, and headed home.

"Did you get your job back?" Bancroft answered.

"Yes, but there's a catch."

"I don't have time for catches."

"Don't you want to know what it is?" Brad dismissed an incoming call from Faye.

"No. You're going to deal with it yourself."

"He wants all of the targets dead in twenty-four hours."

"What?" she exclaimed. "You didn't agree to that, did you? You already know that none of the men on that list you gave me can die. None."

"Either at least one is, or you'll have to pull some strings and fake it. And capture the operative who was sent for that target, so he can't report back to Ralf that he didn't do it."

"Is it one, or is it all?"

"I agreed to all, but I can work with one. I just need it to look like one of them is dead, then I'll demand time with Bergmann. Once I have his attention, I'll get the rest of the information you need."

Then kill him.

"You think you can do that? It's taken you this long to—"

"I can do it. But he's getting impatient. You'll have to fake a death, or my hands are tied."

"Did you not hear me when I told you I can't fake any of these deaths? These men are even more powerful than Giuliano Franco was."

"Looks like we both have our work cut out for us, doesn't it?"

"You need to get this under control, Morris. It's getting out of hand."

"If you can fake one death, I can get the rest of the information from Bergmann."

"You'd better be right."

"I am."

"Don't forget who kept you from prison."

"I haven't."

Bancroft killed the call.

Hopefully Brad was right about getting an audience with Ralf one more time. Otherwise, this would all be for nothing.

Chapter Thirty-One

ZEKE TURNED off the game and leaped up from his chair. He'd been eliminated, and it was because he'd made a dumb move. Couldn't pay attention.

"What's with you today?" Wynn asked. "It's like you forgot how to play."

"Shut up." Zeke didn't want to admit to being scared about asking him if he was the troll.

It seemed a lot less likely after he'd backed Zeke up against Lance at lunch. But even so, he needed to find out who JimBob was.

All at times when Zeke and Wynn were apart.

Today was no different.

"You thinking about Olive?" Wynn gave him a playful shove. "She's cute. I can't believe you're going to the dance with her. I *really* need to start a gaming channel."

"I didn't make my channel to meet girls."

"But it obviously works. You think any of her friends want to go with me?"

"I'm not going to ask." Zeke checked the computer for his stats now that the round had finally ended.

"Some friend you are." Wynn laughed.

It just irritated Zeke.

"What's with you today? Everything is going good for you now."

"Is it?"

"You don't have to worry about Lance anymore *and* you're going to the dance with Olive. Yet you seem pissed at the world. Is fame already getting to your head?"

"I'm *not* famous."

"Did you see all those people in the courtyard? And the way you sent Lance running with his tail between his legs?"

"That doesn't mean—"

"Yes, it does. You finally managed to get popular. You going to be a jerk from now on?"

"I'm not a jerk!"

"Then what's going on?"

Zeke clenched his jaw. Considered his wording. He cared less about offending Wynn now that they were arguing, and he was accusing him of being stuck-up.

"Well?" Wynn narrowed his eyes.

"I want to know who JimBob is!"

"Who? Wait, you mean that stupid troll?"

"Yes, the troll. Who else?"

Wynn's expression softened slightly. "*That's* why you're acting like this?"

"I'm not acting like anything! I lost a round, and you jumped all over my back."

"You didn't just lose *one* round, dude. You've been off your game since we got here today."

Zeke's stomach churned acid. "Tell me what you know about the troll."

"What would I know?"

"That's what I want you to tell me."

"He picked a stupid name, that's about all I know."

"You sure?" Zeke demanded.

"Have you started taking drugs or something?"

"Stop! I need to know the truth."

"What are you *talking* about?" Wynn put his hands up in front of his chest.

"There are a few things that don't make sense about the troll."

"Like what?"

Zeke held up one finger. "For starters, JimBob clearly knows about my dad's real job."

"Okay?"

He held up another finger. "He also never leaves a comment when you're with me."

Confusion crossed Wynn's face, then his eyes widened. "Are you accusing me of being the troll?"

"Should I be?"

"*Are* you?"

Zeke's heart felt like it would explode out of his chest. There was no going back. And if Wynn wasn't the troll, then he'd lose a friend for nothing. And that thought sucked worse than anything else he could think of. Still, he needed to know.

"I just have to find out." Zeke took a deep breath. "I'm not accusing you, but I can't not ask. You're the only one who knows what my dad does."

"You think I'm your stupid troll?"

"I don't know! And for the record, I don't want you to be. But I have to ask."

Wynn's eyes narrowed even further. "How can you say you're not accusing me?"

"Because I'm not! I'm asking."

"How can you even wonder?"

Zeke took measured breaths, his pulse drumming in his ears. "Like I said, too many coincidences. I have to know."

Wynn grabbed his bag. "I'm out of here."

"If you aren't the troll, then why not just say it?"

"Because you should know me better than that, man!"

Zeke blocked the door. "If you walk out of here, you're admitting guilt."

"No. If I leave, it means I'm going home because my best friend doesn't trust me."

"Are you the troll?"

"Move."

Zeke didn't budge. "If you're innocent, just say so."

"I shouldn't *have* to! Out of my way before I give you a black eye."

"Now you're going to hit me?"

"If I have to. Your choice."

Zeke crossed his arms. "I'm not going anywhere until you say you aren't the troll. That's *your* choice."

Wynn's nostrils flared. "Of course I'm not the troll, you idiot!"

"You're not?"

"No!"

Zeke's muscles relaxed. "That's a relief."

"Move. I'm outta here."

"You're still leaving?"

"Duh. You thought I could turn on you like that? I'm gone."

"I had to ask. Don't you see that?"

Wynn's expression tightened. "No. You should've *known*."

"Nobody else knows."

"Other than all of his assassin friends? And your family?"

"Now you're accusing someone in my family of being JimBob?"

Wynn tried to get around him. "It wasn't me. That's all I know."

"Why didn't you just say so before?"

"Because I couldn't believe you'd be so dumb as to accuse me."

"I told you, I wasn't *accusing* you."

"Right. You were asking me. Same difference. Move."

Zeke stood taller. "You'd do the same thing."

"I said, move."

"No."

"Fine. I'll climb out the window, then."

"From the second story?"

"How do you think I get out of my house half the time?" Wynn spun around and marched toward the window.

"Stop!"

Wynn turned around.

"I'm glad it wasn't you."

"Great." He spun back toward the window.

"Stay."

"Why? So you can accuse me of something else? No thanks."

"Don't let this get between us. We've been friends since we were little."

Wynn whipped back around. "And that's exactly why you should've known better! I'd never do anything like that to you. Don't you realize that I'd have stood with you against Lance even if nobody else did? Most of those people didn't give one lick about you before you had your channel. But I did."

Zeke's heart sank. "You're right. I'm sorry. I should've known."

"Exactly." Wynn's brows furrowed.

"Go, if you want." Zeke moved from the door. "I can't blame you for hating me."

It took him a moment to realize his former friend hadn't moved.

"What are you waiting for?"

"Nothing." Wynn flung his bag on the bed.

Zeke tilted his head. "What do you mean?"

"I'm not going anywhere."

"Why not?"

"Because you're honestly sorry."

"What?"

"Everyone makes mistakes, and like you said, I'm not willing to throw our friendship away over something so stupid. And for the record, even thinking that I *might* be the troll is really stupid. I'd never do that to you. Got it?"

Zeke nodded yes, hardly able to believe Wynn wasn't storming away.

Wynn tapped on the keyboard. "You gonna do another round, or what?"

"So, we're really still friends?"

"Of course. Start playing before people think you've lost your groove."

"Uh, okay."

"You're going to play like normal now, right? Now that you know I'm obviously not the troll?"

Zeke nodded and sat at his desk.

It was a relief to know his friend wasn't the troll.

But who was?

Chapter Thirty-Two

BRAD RUBBED his temples and locked his office door. He'd been up most of the night. Bancroft had pulled off a miracle, faked the death of a European head of state and captured the assassin who'd been sent to do the job.

Now it was Brad's turn to do the miraculous.

Today was the day he would kill Ralf Bergmann. He'd put the hours into preparations to make sure nothing went wrong. Bancroft had gotten him a twenty-minute appointment with his time-stingy boss.

Twenty minutes wasn't a long time, but it was far more than he needed to pull a trigger. Or dig a blade into flesh. The actual act wasn't the problem.

It was everything else, as had already been proven twice.

But this time, he had everything ready. Even though he was tired, he was focused, driven. A man on a mission. It had been thirty years in the making.

Nothing would stop him this time.

He had every move, every word perfectly orchestrated.

Once he arrived at the Bergmann house, he would be alone with the man.

He wouldn't hesitate.

Brad went to his room and put on the agent's wire. Texted her to let her know he would be leaving in a few minutes. Turned on the wire so he wouldn't have to think about it when he got there. The less on his mind, the better.

His focus was getting Ralf to talk more about his empire before he pulled the trigger — in self-defense, of course. Then he'd say whatever he had to in order to convince Bancroft there was no other way.

He'd planned everything out so well, he had half a dozen ways the scenario could play out. And each time, he was the innocent one.

Brad knocked on Hadley's door, waited, then opened it.

The room was empty. She must've gone out again. He'd told her not to disturb him unless it was urgent, so she'd probably taken off without a word. Better not be with that Rick guy.

He'd have to worry about that later.

Once Ralf was dead.

He tested the wire.

Bancroft texted him that it was working.

Perfect.

Brad checked the time. If he left right then, he would get there slightly too early.

Better early than late. He hurried downstairs and, out of habit, waved to Faye in the salon. But it was dark.

Right. She was at some kind of training for the day.

He went to the kitchen and made a fresh cup of coffee. Nothing like caffeine to counter-balance his fatigue. Hope-fully, it wouldn't go the other way and make him jittery.

Brad hesitated before taking a sip. He couldn't risk his hands being even the slightest bit shaky. Not when he needed fine-tuned precision.

He dumped the liquid down the sink. Definitely the right choice.

Now to get down to business.

Brad took a deep breath, mentally went over his plans again, and put on his coat and shoes. Checked his weapons, the wire.

Everything was set. The old man wouldn't see it coming.

Brad's mouth curved up as he twisted the knob. Excited butterflies danced in his stomach. It reminded him of being a kid on Christmas Day.

He opened the door, anticipating the fresh spring air and warm sunshine.

Ralf stood on the porch, staring Brad in the eyes.

"What are you doing here?" Brad exclaimed.

His boss only smirked.

"I was just heading over to your place."

"You'd like that, wouldn't you?" Ralf stepped forward.

Brad blocked the doorway.

"Something the matter?"

"Why are you here?"

Ralf moved even closer. "We have something to discuss, don't we?"

"Not here."

"What's wrong with talking here?"

Brad struggled to find the words. None of this meshed with what he'd spent so much time painstakingly planning. "If we're talking business, we should go somewhere private."

Ralf looked at his watch. "Time's ticking. Let's do this."

Everything started spinning around him. Brad couldn't kill in his own home. Not in the place where his family lived. Not when his mom could walk in with Luna at any moment.

Why was Ralf here?

He couldn't possibly know about Brad's plan, could he?

That was impossible. Nobody knew. Only Brad.

"Something the matter?" Ralf grinned.

He looked like the devil himself.

It sent a shiver down Brad's spine.

"Short on words? Or should we go back to the demotion?"

Brad hoped Bancroft was listening to this. If this went sideways, she was supposed to be ready with backup.

But if she had to rescue him, his shot at Ralf would be gone forever.

He either needed to improvise and do the deed here at home, or he needed to wait.

Again.

No. His father's murder had to be avenged.

He would have to do it here.

There would be no way to hide it from Bancroft.

At least Brad could still work it so that he looked like the victim. Self-defense. Same plan, but at home instead of at Ralf's.

He could do this.

"Are we going in?" Ralf asked. "Or should I leave?"

Brad stepped inside and waved his boss in.

Ralf had no idea it would be the last place he would ever see.

Chapter Thirty-Three

HADLEY STEPPED out of the bubble bath and wrapped a soft towel around her. The aromatic soap and soak had been just what she'd needed after a hard day of virtual school. Even though a tough day online wasn't nearly as bad as a good day in the school building, it was still stressful. And the tub was just down the hall.

No dealing with busy hallways and loud kids. No more putting up with kids who didn't practice their lines for the play until the last minute.

Actually, she did kind of miss that. Not so much the lazy people, but being in the plays. Practicing, performing, singing. All of it. Especially the applause, laughter, and cheers of the live audience. Few things were more thrilling than that.

She held the towel tightly, closed her eyes, and thought of her best ovations over the years. It almost made her wish she could go back.

Lucy's words ran through her mind — virtual school kids could take part in the plays, too.

No. Even if she only went to school for that, she would

still have to face Ellie. And everyone who thought she had murdered Nate.

She sighed at the thought of Ellie, who still hadn't bothered calling her. So much for being sorry about the way she'd treated Hadley.

Murder. As if. It had been an accident.

Not to mention the fact that someone who had done far worse was in jail for Nate's death, even though there was no body.

She shoved all those thoughts from her mind, wrapped her hair in a towel, and went to her bedroom.

Her phone showed a missed call from Ellie.

Hadley stared in disbelief. Closed and opened her eyes.

It rang again and she answered it.

"Ellie?"

"You picked up."

Hadley would know that voice anywhere. "Lucy said you wanted to talk."

"Can we talk in person?"

"Aren't you in school?" Hadley asked.

"I'm at lunch."

"You want me to come over there?"

"We could meet somewhere. I have a free period after this, so I have time."

Hadley looked at her reflection — wrapped in a towel, skin still crimson from the bath. "I haven't gotten ready yet. You'd have to be back at school before I could meet."

"I could come to your house while you get ready. You don't need makeup for me."

Except that they weren't friends anymore. Things had changed. She kept her thoughts to herself.

"Are you there?" Ellie asked.

"Give me twenty minutes." That was all Hadley needed to get dressed and apply makeup these days. She wouldn't bother doing anything with her hair. It could air dry.

"You'll open the door if I knock?"

"Yeah." Hadley opened her closet and started flipping through her clothes. "But first tell me what this is about."

"Didn't Lucy tell you?"

"I want to hear it from you."

"Okay. I get that." A beat of silence passed. "I didn't treat you very well. Not like a friend should, much less a best friend. I want to apologize. But in person."

"Why can't you do that over the phone?"

"Because it isn't very personal."

"Says the girl who dumped Travis by text."

"You aren't Travis."

Hadley's heart hadn't stopped racing. It hardly seemed possible this was actually happening. She couldn't let go of the feeling that it could be a trap — that Ellie actually had ulterior motives for wanting to come over.

"I don't blame you for not trusting me," Ellie said. "I wouldn't trust me, either, after how I treated you. Instead of giving you sympathy after your boyfriend *died*, I only thought of myself. How horrible is that? I deserve the 'worst best friend' award."

She didn't disagree.

"I'm really sorry, Hadley."

Hadley sighed. Tried to find the words.

"I have more I want to say, but I'd rather say it in person."

"You really want to make up?"

"Yeah. And I understand if you can't forgive me right away. At least let me apologize, and then we can take the next step when you're ready."

"You're not mad at me?" Hadley asked. "You sure were before I switched to virtual school."

"I was a jerk. I mean, I was definitely hurt, but that's still no excuse. My being hurt was nothing compared to what you had to be going through. And I'm sure I only made things worse for you."

"You could say that."

"If I could take it all back, I totally would. But since I can't, I want to try and make it up to you."

"Make it up? What do you mean?"

"Whatever it takes, I want to make things right. Get them back to where they used to be. I know it won't be right away, but I'm going to start by being the friend you need. I'll be there in twenty minutes — and for the record, I don't care what you look like. Don't bother getting dressed for me. I hear you banging hangers around."

Hadley nearly smiled. "Well, I'm in a towel now. I'm not staying in that all day."

"Why not? You could always start a trend."

"Not with this." She *had* begun several trends at school, but never anything so ridiculous. "I'll see you in twenty."

"I won't be late. And I'm bringing chocolate." Ellie ended the call.

Hadley stared at the blank screen for a moment, hardly able to believe the conversation they'd just had. Maybe Lucy was right.

And maybe she was wrong. What if this was all a trick?

Hadley opened her photos app and found pictures of her and Ellie, laughing and having fun together.

It *would* be nice to go back to those days. She couldn't get Duke back, but maybe she could get her best friend back.

She quickly got dressed, ran a brush through her hair, and applied mascara and gloss. It was all she had time for if she wanted to eat before Ellie arrived. And if she really was coming with chocolate, Hadley would need something in her stomach first.

Downstairs, there were some strange noises coming from the direction of the living room.

She couldn't figure out what they were. Low voices, maybe?

But who would be talking? No one else was home except Dad.

He was probably watching TV. That would explain the voices.

She headed downstairs to see.

He stood near the back door with an overly tanned, bald guy with his back to Hadley.

Dad's eyes widened, and his face paled. He flicked his head quickly, obviously telling her to leave.

The other man turned, his expression registering shock.

He held a gun.

Hadley turned and ran back upstairs.

She needed to warn Ellie away.

Chapter Thirty-Four

BRAD LUNGED FOR RALF, who had raced after Hadley.

He wrapped his arms around him and yanked him to a stop.

Ralf spun around and hit Brad in the side of the head with the gun.

The sound reverberated in his head. Stars danced before his eyes.

Brad stumbled back.

Ralf ran toward the hallway.

"Leave her alone! This is between us."

Ralf spun around. "Is it?"

"Of course. She has nothing to do with this."

"Nothing?" His face contorted into a scowl.

"What would a seventeen-year-old girl have to do with anything?"

"The same one who infiltrated the Slippery Fish?"

"It was a part-time job, and she quit on her first day!" Brad reached for him.

Ralf whipped around and pursued Hadley. "We need to talk, little girl."

Fury tore through Brad. "Don't listen to him, Hadley!"

Brad caught up with Ralf, squeezed his shoulders, and yanked him back. "Touch her, and you will die."

Ralf swung the gun at him, this time missing. "If you want your job back, this is the wrong way to go about it."

"I don't care about that now." Brad shoved him against the wall, knocking over a framed family photo. The corner scraped Ralf near the eye, and blood dripped from the cut.

"You were begging pretty hard over the phone. That's why I thought it best to come over before our appointment." Ralf regained his hold on the trigger and aimed the muzzle between Brad's eyes.

Brad's stomach dropped. He couldn't let Ralf kill him while Hadley could hear.

She'd already been through too much. That could send her over the edge.

Again.

Ralf pressed the cold metal to his forehead. "You think I'm not onto you?"

"About what?"

"Don't play stupid with me."

"What do you think I'm doing?" Brad demanded.

"Trying to destroy my empire. It's because of you that Kurt's behind bars."

"You think so?"

"I *know* so."

Kurt had found a way to get a message to his father. At least Brad was getting this on the wire — Bancroft was listening in real time. Kurt would lose any privileges her people had granted him.

But that was little consolation with a gun shoved against his skull.

And his daughter in the house.

If Ralf killed him, he couldn't protect his daughter.

Hopefully Bancroft had a team on the way. Or maybe Hadley had called the cops, if she had her phone on her. And when didn't she?

But she could be too scared to think of that. Or too worried that talking would alert Ralf to her hiding spot. And Bancroft could be distracted.

There could be no help coming. He needed to assume it was so.

Killing Ralf was more important than ever. Avenging his father's death was now of little consequence. Dad was already gone. Hadley was not.

Brad reached for the gun.

Ralf blocked his arm, keeping the weapon in place. He was still against the wall.

Brad glanced to the left, opening his mouth as if to speak.

Ralf turned to look, giving Brad his opportunity.

He pulled away from the old man's hold and raced in the other direction.

"Get back here!" Ralf's footsteps thundered behind him.

Brad reached for his gun, finally having the chance.

"Stop!"

Bang!

A bullet exploded in the wall next to his head.

Ralf had barely missed. On purpose?

Brad yanked out his weapon and aimed it at Ralf. "You need to leave my house."

His nostrils flared. "I don't leave loose threads."

"Neither do I."

Both men stood there, guns aimed at each other, staring one another down.

Brad's mind raced. He could shoot, but risked Ralf also pulling the trigger faster.

He also wanted to let Ralf know that he knew about him murdering his dad.

But he had to stop him from harming Hadley.

He applied pressure on the trigger, but not enough to do anything. There was no going back.

"What are you waiting for?" Ralf snarled. "Shoot me!"

"Why did you order my father's death?" The gun shook in Brad's grip.

The corners of Ralf's mouth curved up.

"Why?"

Ralf laughed. Then he lunged for Brad, knocking Brad's gun arm upward, so fast that Brad barely got off a shot that went way over Ralf's head. He pivoted and ducked under a punch, then shoved his boss against the wall.

His fingers found the pressure point on Ralf's forearm, and the man dropped his weapon with an agonized grunt.

"Tell me!" Brad grabbed the collar of Ralf's shirt. Shoved him again. Forced the gun to his temple.

"Don't you already know?"

"I want to hear it from you!"

Ralf wiped spit from his cheek. "How long did it take you to find out? Did you already know before you were hired?"

"Why did you kill him?"

"He was going to walk away. *Nobody* leaves unless I decide they do."

Everything took on a red hue. Brad struggled to focus. "He had a family!"

"Too bad you're going to meet the same tragic end as him — and you have even more kids to mourn you."

"Who has the gun to whose head?"

Ralf body-slammed him.

Brad stumbled back. Kept the weapon aimed at the old man.

Pulled the trigger.

Missed by an inch. Another hole in a wall.

Shot again. Missed.

The old man flew at him. They both crashed to the floor.

Brad hit his head on the coffee table on the way down.

More stars.

This was not good.

Ralf flew at him, seeming to come from above.

Barely able to see around the dancing stars, Brad rolled over to the other side.

"Oof!" Ralf landed at an odd angle. Couldn't be good at his age.

A hand grabbed Brad's face, nails digging into his flesh.

Brad kicked and flailed his arms, white flaring at the edges of his vision.

He couldn't give up. Not when Ralf would go after Hadley next.

He kicked Ralf with all the force he had. Pulled himself up. Used the couch to steady himself. Looked around for his gun.

The edge of the grip stuck out from under the far end of the couch.

Brad tripped as he took a step toward it.

On the other side of the couch, Ralf fumbled as he struggled to stand.

As Brad reached his weapon, his finger slid, and he accidentally pushed the gun further underneath the furniture.

Grasping the armrest, Ralf sauntered around to Brad's side.

Brad tried to focus on him, to ignore the stars floating between them.

Needed to distract him.

Pointed behind the old man. "Hadley, no!"

Ralf looked up toward the stairs.

Brad squatted down, a rush of blood making him feel lightheaded on top of everything else. Reached around for his weapon. Felt the trigger guard. Looped his pinky around it. Pulled it out.

Stood quickly. Another rush of blood.

Must have a concussion.

Not that it would stop him.

Wrangled his hand around the grip. Placed his finger around the trigger.

Ralf spun around. "You can't fool me that easily, Morris."

"Already did." He aimed, managing to keep his hold steady and work around the stars. Moved his finger on the trigger, ready to pull.

Hadley appeared in the hallway — somehow she'd managed to get downstairs during the scuffle, without either of them noticing. Her hands went to her mouth.

Brad froze.

He couldn't kill Ralf in front of his daughter.

Even if he'd ordered the hit on his dad.

Even though she herself had accidentally taken a life.

No. He would need to take Ralf down with non-lethal means.

Let the justice system deal with him, making him pay for his many crimes.

That was the right thing to do.

Even if impossibly hard.

Brad turned to Ralf. "It's over."

Chapter Thirty-Five

HADLEY STARED at her dad pointing a gun at the bald man, who was waving a BlueBlade knife around like a drunken maniac.

Her heart sank.

She had to do something.

Dad waved her away.

Hadley shook her head.

He narrowed his eyes, a clear warning.

Not wanting to distract him, she retreated to the hallway. But no way was she going to leave him to deal with that crazy guy on his own. She hurried through the kitchen, tiptoeing and holding her breath, stopping only to grab a steak knife.

She peeked through the other door.

Now Dad was on the floor, wrestling with the guy.

It was impossible to tell who had the advantage. Both the knife and the gun had been flung to the side, obviously lost in the strife.

Her heart felt like it would explode out of her chest.

She took a deep breath, clutched the knife close, and crept over.

With Dad on top, it would be impossible to stab the other man. And she couldn't risk hurting Dad.

She'd have to wait.

Dad cried out.

The bald guy flipped him onto his back.

Hadley raised arm, ready to slice into the leathery skin. Might be a challenge.

A hand landed on her shoulder.

She gasped, and turned around, holding the blade even higher.

Rick stood back, his hands raised. "It's just me."

Relief washed through her. She lowered the knife.

"Thanks for leaving the front door unlocked," he whispered. "Let me handle this."

Hadley nodded, and handed him the weapon.

He shook his head and leaped over to them.

Did he think he could take care of this unarmed?

Rick pulled something gray and rectangular from his jacket pocket. Aimed it at the bald guy.

The man jerked around like he was having a seizure. Fell to the floor, moaning.

Dad sat up. "Who are you?"

Rick leaned close to him. "Your eyes don't look like they're dilating normally."

"*Who* are you?"

Rick turned to Hadley. "Is he usually this pale?"

She hurried over. "No."

Rick turned back to Dad. "I think you might have a concussion. I'm going to call for a medic."

Dad stood up, clinging to the backside of the love seat. "You never said who you are."

Rick was already on the phone.

Hadley offered her arm for support. "Dad, that's Rick. I didn't know who else to call after I saw you and that guy aiming guns at each other."

"You could've called the cops."

"That's what he told me to do."

"Did you?"

"Yes."

Rick turned back toward them. "The police are almost here, and an ambulance is on its way."

Dad crossed his arms. "You're the guy who's seeing my underage daughter?"

"Dad!" Hadley exclaimed. "He just saved your life!"

Rick took a deep breath. "It isn't like that, sir."

Dad's stance relaxed slightly. "What is it, then?"

"We're friends," Hadley interjected.

Rick looked at her. "Remember the other day, I told you I needed to tell you something? And then I got called to work?"

Hadley nodded, her stomach churning. She wasn't going to like whatever he was about to say.

"Well? I take it you weren't hired by Ralf." Dad motioned toward the old guy passed out on the carpet.

"No." Rick glanced back and forth between her and Dad. "By Agent Bancroft, actually."

Hadley stepped away from him. "What?"

"At first, I was just watching the house — making sure you were all safe. But then after Hadley got the job at the car wash, I was assigned to protect her. I attempted take out the car pursuing her, but was unable to do so without putting her in danger. As soon as it was over, I immediately rushed out to help get her to safety."

Hadley's heart pounded. "You mean I'm just a *job* to you?"

"No, not at all." He held her gaze, his eyes intense. "We're definitely friends."

"What does that mean?" Dad demanded.

Rick turned to him. "It means your daughter is a very special person. I never get involved with my clients, but after the accident, I had to get her out of the car, out of the street. And as we hid in the store, I grew increasingly concerned for her. I watched outside the hospital each day, and had to check in personally once she was home. We have a connection from the night of the accident."

Hadley wanted to ask more questions, but didn't dare with Dad there.

Footsteps sounded in the hall.

Five policemen filled the living room. Two paramedics followed them.

Rick pointed to Dad. "Over here. I think he has a concussion."

Hadley pointed to Dad's attacker. "He tried to kill my dad. Shot a gun at him and everything."

"Who is he?" asked of the cops.

"I'm not sure. Everything happened so fast."

"Okay. I'll see what your dad can tell me. He's the one with the possible concussion, right?"

"Yeah."

The policeman went over to Dad, who sat on the couch, being examined by two medics.

Hadley turned to Rick. "So, I'm your client?"

"Technically, yes."

"How is it not? Do you take all your clients to the festival?"

He shook his head. "No. Like I said, usually I never meet them. But you … you're special."

Her face flamed. "Wait. You know about my stay in the hospital?"

"It isn't something to be ashamed of. Plenty of people use those services after a traumatic event."

She clenched her fists. "What else do you know about me?"

"Mostly what you've told me. My job was to keep you and your family safe, and I was only given details pertinent to that."

"Pertinent, huh?"

He nodded, amusement in his eyes. "Yes. And I haven't let anything get in the way of keeping you safe."

Hadley glanced around at the mess in the living room. "If you were so busy keeping us safe, how come you weren't right here when I called for help? Why didn't you see that jerk when he came inside?"

"I was on lunch, which is allowed. Besides, I beat the police here, didn't I?"

She couldn't deny that. "True. So, what now?"

"I'll continue protecting you and your family until Agent Bancroft believes I'm no longer needed."

"And after that?"

He took her hand and led her to a corner where they had a little privacy. "Do you mean between us?"

"Of course."

He nodded and looked deep in thought. "I'd be lying if I said your father doesn't worry me."

"He's harmless."

"He's an assassin."

"You're a bodyguard."

Rick chuckled, then squeezed her hand. "I'd really like to keep getting to know you. But we can only be friends while I'm working for your family."

"I like that idea. It gives me time to work through some stuff. Do you know about that, too?"

"Your previous boyfriend?"

Hadley nodded, barely able to keep looking at Rick. She was saved from having to say anything, because a police officer came over.

The officer looked at Hadley. "If you don't need to be checked out by the paramedics, I'm going to take your statement."

"I wasn't hurt at all."

"I'm glad to hear it. Let's go to the kitchen, where it's quieter."

She nodded.

Rick squeezed her hand.

At least he understood her need to go slow. Whatever would happen between them, if anything, there would be time to figure it out.

Chapter Thirty-Six

"THAT'S A WRAP." Brad wiped sweat from his brow and stepped off the mat, looking around his new self-defense studio. "Good session, ladies. You're all doing great."

Catching their breath, his mom, Faye, Hadley, and Luna all gathered their things now that their private lesson was over.

Faye kissed his cheek. "You're doing great too — you're such a talented teacher."

He put his arm around her. "It's easy when the students are so eager to learn."

"Thanks, Dad." Hadley smiled as she pulled some hair from her face. "I really appreciate you teaching us self-defense."

"Believe me, it's my pleasure."

"I probably won't be home when you get there. I'm going to take a quick shower, then rush off to rehearsal. After that, I'm spending the night at Ellie's."

"Again?"

Hadley laughed. "Of course."

His mom came over, her new engagement ring

catching the studio's bright lights. "You'll be there tomorrow, won't you? Richard and I will be over tomorrow night for our weekly dinner."

Hadley kissed her cheek. "Wouldn't miss it."

Brad's mom turned to him as Hadley hurried away. "Is she still seeing that nice young man?"

"Rick." Brad nodded. "They claim to still be just friends, but I have a feeling once she turns eighteen their status will change."

"Good for her, finding such a nice boy."

"He's okay."

Faye shoved him. "He's great for her, you have to admit."

"I don't have to admit anything." He especially wasn't going to admit that he actually liked the guy. Rick was twice the man Duke had ever been, promising never to go behind Brad and Faye's backs about anything. Also, there wasn't as much of an age gap between them as there had been with Duke. That helped to set his mind at ease.

After saying goodbye to his mom, Brad went to the counter and got everything ready for the next day.

"Any more sessions tonight?" Faye asked, helping Luna with her hair.

"Nope. But I'll have to be here early tomorrow. Saturday morning is a popular time for self-defense classes. I'm going to need to add an extra class before the summer starts."

She wrapped her arms around him. "I'm so proud of you. You could've fallen apart after BlueBlade went under, but you didn't. Now look at you, putting your skills to good use."

"I'm just glad I can finally help make this world a safer place. I thought I was before, but now I actually am."

Luna tugged on his arm. "Can we pick up pizza, Daddy? Or teriyaki? Or anything? Please?"

He snickered, and turned to Faye. "What do you think?"

"I'm all for not cooking after the workout you just gave me." She winked and kissed him. "How about Luna and I pick something up while you finish here? Then we'll meet at home."

"Sounds good. Will Zeke be home, or is he out with Olive again?"

"They have another school dance tonight." Faye gave him a quick kiss. "See you in a few."

"Bye." He waved as they left, and wandered through the studio, making sure nothing else needed to be done before the next morning's classes.

Everything looked good.

Just like his life, amazingly enough.

Agent Bancroft had so much on Ralf and Kurt, they would never see the outside of prison walls again, thanks to the coded book of transactions whose location Brad had provided. In addition to all of the criminal activity surrounding the operation — five cells in total — Ralf had also been behind Zeke's troll.

Nobody else knew about Brad's time as an assassin. His secret was safe, and he had full immunity.

In addition to that, the agent had managed to keep Brad and the other assassins out of any prosecutions as long as they agreed to never participate in any illegal killings again. Scott and another guy had joined her agency. Brad and the others had all gone other directions.

Brad had been uninspired at first, but then when he started teaching the ladies in his house a few self-defense moves, the idea had sparked.

Now he was busy teaching classes Tuesday through

Saturday. He and Faye both took Sundays and Mondays off, enjoying each other's company. Her salon was doing so well she was looking into hiring part-time help. Something Brad would have to consider soon, if this kept up.

The kids and his mom were all busy with their own things. Hadley had started performing in plays after making up with Ellie, and now she was attending school in person again. Zeke was still obsessed with his video games, but not to the point where he avoided social activities. Even Luna, who was following in her sister's footsteps, had landed the role of Lead Candy Cane in the holiday play.

His mom had moved back into her home shortly after Brad's confrontation with Ralf. Now engaged, she and Richard were looking to purchase a home together near her son. And he seemed to be helping her manage her condition better than Brad and Faye had been able to.

Yes, everything was going great.

Brad couldn't ask for anything more.

What To Read Next...

April 5th has always been a bad day for Clara. This year it's the day when her husband Shane was arrested for a 20 year old crime: the murder of Clara's best friend in high school. But nothing is as it seems as Clara tries clear her husband's name, even as she finds more reasons not to trust him.

Pick up your copy of Lost and Found today!

A Quick Favor...

If you enjoyed this book, please take a moment to write a short review on your favorite online bookstore so other readers can enjoy it, too.

Thanks so much!

About the Authors

Stacy Claflin is a USA Today bestselling thriller author who has published more than 75 novels, including Girl in Trouble and The Perfect Death. She has always been curious about the human mind, and in her quest to learn more, she earned a degree in Psychology. Her favorite course was Abnormal Behavior, which has been useful in writing fiction.

Her love for thrillers goes back to her early childhood when she fell in love with Unsolved Mysteries and America's Most Wanted. When Stacy was five, she got mad at a babysitter who wouldn't let her watch the evening news. These days, she spends her free time listening to true crime podcasts or watching documentaries on the subject.

She has been telling stories for as long as she can remember, and as child would often get into trouble for trying to convince friends her wild tales were true. Now she puts her creativity to better use by writing page-turning stories that leave readers begging for more.

Nolon King writes fast-paced psychological thrillers set in the glitzy world of entertainment's power players with a bold, insightful voice. He's not afraid to explore the darker side of human nature through stories featuring families torn apart by secrets and lies.

Nolon loves to write about big questions and moral

quandaries. How far would you go to cover up an honest mistake? Would you destroy your career to protect your family? How much of your soul would you sell to get the life of your dreams? Would you cheat on your husband to keep your children safe? Would you give in to a stalker's demands to save your marriage?